# Pavlov's Dog

# Pavlov's Dog

David Kurman

Winchester, UK
Washington, USA

First published by Roundfire Books, 2017
Roundfire Books is an imprint of John Hunt Publishing Ltd., Laurel House, Station Approach,
Alresford, Hants, SO24 9JH, UK
office1@jhpbooks.net
www.johnhuntpublishing.com
www.roundfire-books.com

For distributor details and how to order please visit the 'Ordering' section on our website.

Text copyright: David Kurman 2016

ISBN: 978 1 78535 613 1
978 1 78535 614 8 (ebook)
Library of Congress Control Number: 2016954758

A CIP catalogue record for this book is available from the British Library.

Design: Stuart Davies

Printed and bound by CPI Group (UK) Ltd, Croydon, CR0 4YY, UK

We operate a distinctive and ethical publishing philosophy in all
areas of our business, from our global network of authors to
production and worldwide distribution.

For Sheila: everything I do is just an elaborate ruse
to try to impress you.

"We are what we pretend to be."
—Kurt Vonnegut (*Mother Night*)

# Chapter 1

Dawn crept in like a ninja in feety pajamas.

Three shrill rings called out through the silence as if sending an elementary Morse code: *Ding! Ding! Ding!* = "Come! Feed! Me!"

One lone sock with a hole in it so large it might as well have been a legwarmer answered the call, dragging behind it its half-conscious, half-dreaming, half-sober owner. Sure, that doesn't add up correctly, but Stan Pavlov wasn't the kind of man who let something as trivial as the laws of mathematics define him.

He cherished these moments, even standing there in the freezing kitchen, naked bar one dysfunctional sock, the other, God knew where—probably in the microwave—knowing Sarah was tucked up in bed, wrapped tightly in the sheets like a five-foot-three-inch tamale.

Once again, a perky paw the color of melted chocolate reached up and announced his presence on the bell—*Ding! Ding! Ding!*—bringing Stan back to the task at hand. It was quiet moments like these when his only responsibility was to determine what flavor dog food to pour that he could close his eyes and forget that . . . well, just forget.

Sarah was finally up and about. She would never know it, but by a million-to-one chance her struggle to liberate herself from the sheets caused her long brown hair, which normally bobbed and teased at her waistline, to become tied in a perfect double timber hitch knot, and so expertly so, that it could have earned her a merit badge.

Upon hearing the creak of the third-to-last stair, Stan and the dog came running to greet her; if Stan had a tail he would have wagged it. He genuinely had affection for her, but he had even greater fondness for what she represented: no more going to friends' weddings alone, no more cold December nights staring at

1

the ceiling in despair, no more masturbating to the Home Shopping Network.

They shared a prototypical New York apartment; it was roughly the square footage of a small dish towel. But the apartment held sacred memories of building a life with his dog. And then there was Sarah; in his self-constructed world of lies and deception, her unwavering truth kept him grounded; she was real. Even the sight of her name, written out in longhand, nearly made him weep, the way the letters dipped and looped, bobbed and weaved, every other letter standing tall and proud like a mad, majestic mountain range: *Sarah*. . .

When it was obvious that there was no more time to stall, and the inevitability of having to face the day sank in, Sarah gave him a soft peck on the cheek and handed him a small brown bag with his lunch—something she found hibernating at the back of the fridge that didn't fight back when she gingerly flicked it.

As Stan clattered his way out the door with his array of stage props, she gently held up her hand and he stopped in his tracks, as if on command.

"Stan! Wait a second. Wish me luck. I have that big meeting today, remember?"

He didn't remember. In fact, he had no idea what her job actually was. It was just one of those things that he never thought to ask, and when it did occur to him, it was far too late in the relationship to admit to such a glaring omission in his knowledge. So he just kept bluffing and kept his questions vague. He was far from selfish but close to self-centered; as an actor, essentially, he had to be. It was his fatal character flaw, he knew, that his primary focus had been, since a very young age, an unrelenting drive toward his acting career; and in this pursuit, he was as single-minded and dogged as gravity itself.

Stan considered, took a moment to think how best to deliver his lines, and said with as much conviction as he could muster: "Good . . . you know . . . good luck. Today. Good luck today."

As he left, and Sarah bolted and locked the door behind him, she said in voice so soft that she barely heard it herself, "Don't get fired, dear."

\* \* \*

He had been with the Reflex Players Ensemble for six months and was still waiting to get a lead part. Up until now, he had been playing the more nuanced character roles. Roles that often had numbers in them: waiter #3, townsfolk #9, tree #18. Or roles without a name, just defined by their job, like: Policeman, Guard, Curtain Puller.

When the company performed *Hamlet*, he had grand illusions of, perhaps, getting cast as Rosencrantz or Guildenstern, characters who, like him, were easily forgettable, victims of the larger machinations of others. But instead, he had been asked to take on the challenging portrayal of Curtain on the Left. Disappointed, he had hung in there all the same—*and* been on time for every rehearsal—hanging suspended from a pole like a limp, fat, talentless Jesus.

He was aware that what he lacked in talent, he had to make up for in excruciating persistence and punctuality. Someday, some remarkable day, it would all click because . . . well, because it had to. He had nothing else to fall back on.

In theory, Stan had an agent who was supposed to help him negotiate with the theater's artistic director and get him more work. But since that fateful day they met—ten years ago—he hadn't seen or heard from him since. Checking the milk carton for his picture became a regular habit and one that didn't seem weird after the first five or six years. Occasionally, Stan would imagine seeing his agent's slightly out-of-focus photo with the ensuing caption: "Nigel G. Van Vliet, five-foot-nine, cartoonish blue-black hair, about 200 pounds, probably drunk, last seen intending to call Stan about a job." Nigel, Stan knew, was a very lazy man, a man of big plans and small action. And obviously a man without Stan's phone number.

He arrived at the theater, aware that the space faintly smelled of damp no matter what the season or weather outside. He liked arriving early, before anyone else was there, having the space all to himself, imagining the seats filled, the audience rapt. His fellow actors were friendly, but not friends; he was only really comfortable standing alone onstage on a randomly marked piece of tape, imagining it was placed there just for him.

The production manager coughed quietly to announce his presence. Stan instinctively clenched; the production manager never had good news. His voice was like the incessant buzzing of a wounded summer fly.

"Hey, Stan. Just the person I wanted to see. I've been wanting to ask you a question."

Stan lightly, absently, scratched the back of his hand. "Oh, yes?"

"Yeah, I was just completing your evaluation—"

"Oh?"

"Uh-huh."

The production manager pushed back his glasses firmly, even though they were as far back as they could possibly go. "I thought you'd be the best person to ask this: is 'dumb ass' one word or two?"

"Um, I'm pretty sure it's two words."

"Great. Thanks."

Stan dropped his head and turned to go.

"One more thing. The director wants to see you. Now." Before turning and walking away, he added faintly, sincerely, "Sorry."

Stan shook, trembled, quivered, shivered, and oscillated. He felt like he was about to shit like a Mexican donkey. This was worse than stage fright. This was unemployment fright. The director only wanted to see you if there was trouble, and this wasn't the first time . . .

There was the time Stan accidentally stabbed a fellow actor with a stage sword during a curtain call. There was the time, during a performance of *Macbeth*, he got so caught up in the action that he inadvertently yelled out, "Look out, Duncan!" Then there was the time that he brought down the house; not figuratively of course, but literally, when he accidently knocked down the supporting beam.

And that was just this week.

Stan slowly opened the door; the director's office was a stark reflection of the man: gray, angry, cold. He was sitting slumped over his desk, head in hands, palms in eyes, bile in throat. Without looking up, and in an impressive exhibition of his mime skills, he motioned for Stan to come in, sit down, and shut up.

Stan sat in the timid chair, which wobbled slightly as, like Stan himself, it had very little support.

"Stan . . . are you and Jonathan having any issues?"

"Nooooooooooo. No, no, no, no. No. Not really."

The director spread his hands wide on the table, palms down. "But . . . I understand that you *shot* him."

"It was a faulty prop."

"Twice."

"Well, I just wanted to make sure."

"But there was no gun prop called for in that scene!"

"Hey! Have you ever heard of a little thing called 'improvising'?"

The director closed his bloodshot eyes, gripped the edges of his desk, and tried again.

"Okay . . . I'm not quite sure how to say this. Pavlov, if Shakespeare had known how you would butcher his words, he would have cut off his own fingers and jammed them up his ass. You have the memory of an inebriated mayfly born to a particularly dim-witted family of mayflies. And onstage, you have the body language of a man who has just recently defecated in his own pants."

"Well . . . well . . . if you're going to talk to me like that, then . . . I . . . I quit."

"Get out!"

# Chapter 2

Stan hit the pavement hard, handing his headshot to everyone he could: casting agencies, rep companies, crossing guards, waitstaff. Anyone sitting still long enough for Stan to sneak his headshot under their arm, whether they wanted it or not.

After several weeks of persistence, however, he finally had some breaking news for Sarah and prepared himself with several noisy vocal exercises while poised on his own doorstep. Hearing him, Sarah cracked opened the door, the dog howling in her wake, excited, knowing he was only three quick *dings* away from his dinner.

Hands pressed tight, as if in silent prayer, Sarah squeaked, "So, how did it go? Did you get a part today?"

Stan smiled, dropped a duffel bag hard on the floor, like a wartime sailor just returned home. He hugged her a little tighter than usual to let her know everything would be all right, but he couldn't look her in the eye. "Yeah . . . yeah . . . I did . . . sort of."

Three quick, succinct notes later, and Stan, his back turned to Sarah, immediately tended to the dog.

"What do you mean, exactly? What do you have in that bag?"

Stan stood up, looked down at his itchy feet, and put his hands in his empty pockets. "So . . . I . . . I got a part . . . a job . . . as a . . . it's a giant hotdog costume. I'll be handing out fliers in front of the Dog Pound Bar and Grill. Not exactly *King Lear*, but, you know . . . it's acting . . . in a way . . ."

"Oh. Well, that's great, sweetie. With ketchup or mustard? Or are you going commando?"

Stan let out a long, heavy sigh. Bless Sarah. Her bullshit-o-meter must be well overdue for its fifty-thousand-mile check-up.

"I'm just going to try to make the most of this, you know? I mean, this could lead to bigger and better things. I try to think: in this situation, what would Marlon Brando do?"

Sarah's puppy-dog brown eyes raised themselves up to the ceiling, as if searching for divine inspiration. "Um . . . fire his agent?" she suggested helpfully.

*Very probably*, Stan thought, *very, very probably*. This was the hard part—feeling like he was letting her down. How long could she possibly keep overlooking this? How long before . . . Stan turned to face her. He reached out and desperately gripped both of her hands in his, pulling them toward him. "Sarah, how long have we been together?"

"Four years."

Stan dropped her hands. "Whoa. Really?"

"Yes."

"Are you sure?"

"Yes."

"That just doesn't sound right."

"Stan—"

"I would have believed a year, maybe two, but—"

She roughly grabbed his hands and pulled them toward her this time, looking him intently in the eyes. "Stan, the sympathy train is about to leave the station."

"Right, sorry. Well, my point is . . . well . . . Sarah, you still believe in me, after all this time, don't you? You think . . . you think I'm going to make it someday, right?"

Sarah, still holding his sweaty hands in hers, looked down, away, and eventually found solace in her watch. "Hey, aren't you late for your next audition?"

\* \* \*

Like many, many foolish people before him, Stan had spent several years and tens of thousands of dollars studying liberal arts. He could tell you the difference between Zen Buddhism and traditional Buddhism; the causes and implications of the fall of the Ottoman Empire; what actually made Pablo Picasso's "blue period" blue. His college had utilized some brilliant minds to share with him all this knowledge and more.

What they failed to teach him was how to get a decent-paying job after graduation. He must have been out sick that day.

As Stan and the dog approached the sign-in table, a plucky intern greeted Stan on his arrival with a face that hurt from fake smiling as he accepted Stan's headshot into his outstretched hands as if he were handling a small, hot turd.

The dog, his loyal audition companion, peeked his head over the desk as Stan introduced himself as he did day after day, week after week, rejection after rejection, knowing that any moment, any audition, could be the one. "Hi, I'm Pavlov. Stan Pavlov."

"You're here for the cola commercial?"

"Yes, that's right."

The intern did a quick scan of Stan's headshot credits; Stan rolled and re-rolled his sleeves in nervous anticipation, hoping the intern was too idealistic to know that the place where the truth goes to die is the back of struggling actors' headshots. He wasn't.

"I'm sorry, sir . . . but appearing in court does not count as a performance."

"Yeah, well, you didn't see me that day. I was *really* on—"

"Uh-huh, well, that may be, but . . ."

Fearful that the intern was intent on dismissing him and squishing his creased headshot into the "hell no" pile, Stan was about to argue when the intern locked in on the deep, sad eyes of— "Excuse me, is that your dog?"

"Yeah, I'm sorry, I have to take him with me sometimes."

"Has he ever done any commercial work?"

Stan was sure he had misheard. When the intern continued to look straight through him, Stan realized it wasn't a joke. Pointing a confused finger at the dog, he stammered, "What, you mean . . . you mean, him? He's a dog. He shits outside and humps legs. Well . . . not just *anyone's* leg, I mean—"

"Does he have a reel?"

"A reel? Um . . . no. It's bad enough having one actor in the family."

He laughed weakly and when the intern failed to join in, he laughed extra hard on his behalf. It was the least he could do.

"I see. Well, have a seat. We'll be with you shortly."

Stan backed away, smiling like an escaped mental patient, and nearly curtsied in deference. He had learned long ago that even the most junior person could tip the balance of who got cast.

As he pulled the dog along to a quiet seat in the corner, Stan whispered quietly, "Come on, boy," and as he watched him waddle and flop on the floor, he remembered why he put himself through this humiliation day after day.

He hadn't even been looking to get a dog. He hadn't even been able to keep a fern alive for more than two days. He imagined that if houseplants had post offices, his unflattering picture would be thumbtacked up on a bulletin board in one, with WANTED written beneath it. Without looking for any commitment or responsibility and certainly not love, which he had given up on long ago . . . their eyes had met. It was a shock, a physical shock, like walking straight into a smudgeless glass door that you thought was open.

But now Stan knew, as his fingers danced through the dog's stubby fur, he would never, could never, have a bad day again.

His dog didn't judge, he didn't lie, was incapable of envy, held no ambitions, and could love a well-meaning stranger just as much as he could love his owner. He possessed Christ-like acceptance and forgiveness of practically any human being he would ever meet. He more than satisfied that innocent, instinctive desire for unconditional love, companionship, acceptance, and asked for very little in return.

As Stan nearly wept with the memory of it, daydream-doodling on the back of his headshot folder until his name was called, he thought nothing of seeing the intern jot something down...

# Chapter 3

More times than Stan could count, he wanted nothing more than Sarah's company. When she was the only person on Earth he needed. When he so badly wanted her, times when he needed to unashamedly confide in her, share with her his most intimate, innermost thoughts. When, no matter what the world threw at him, she was all he would ever need to get by.

This was not one of those times.

Which was why, if he wasn't so terrified of the slightest instance of pain, he would have kicked himself for agreeing to meet Sarah in the park. He hated the park. Being outside in the middle of the day, when he knew most people were at their jobs, secure in a paycheck and likely in themselves, only made him anxious.

He shuffled toward her slowly, softly, as if hoping she wouldn't see him and he could just sneak on by. Through a crack in the trees, as yet unseen, Stan watched Sarah and the dog speak without saying a word, share a common, knowing smile.

He never wanted to move, just wanted this moment to linger on and on. Sharing the dog, he realized, having him embedded in their lives, was so much better than having children; the dog would never grow up, he would always need them to take care of him, he would be eternally dependent, eternally grateful; they would all be frozen in these roles forever.

But then, his cover was broken. She just happened to turn too far in his direction and caught him, staring, dreaming, smiling. As he approached them, Stan leaned forward for an anticipated kiss, which never materialized.

"So . . . how was your first day of being a professional hotdog?"

"Good. Good. Went very well."

Sarah bobbed and weaved, trying to get Stan to make eye

contact, "Oh, yeah?"

Stan kicked an innocent pebble, put his hands behind his back, as if they might give him away. "Yeah, yup. Very well."

"Really?"

"Oh, yeah. Very, very well. I . . . uh . . . I quit, though."

"They fired you?"

"Yeah. Yeah, they did."

How could he explain? How could he explain that the world of acting was fickle, that chemistry with a role was something that just happened and couldn't be manufactured, that he was just a lost man still looking for his proper place?

Stan bent halfway to meet the dog, who jumped up to lick him, passionately, as if they had been separated by decades and oceans, rather than having just seen each other earlier that morning. "They said I wasn't very convincing as a hotdog. They just weren't buying it. They did say they thought I'd make an exceptional chicken finger. Or even a cheeseburger. So, you know. There's that."

Stan knew Sarah was trying to not let him see her laugh, but her attempt to turn it into a throat-clearing cough wasn't fooling anyone, probably not even the dog. A terrible doubt was angrily eating up his insides; he grabbed her hands, as if afraid she might turn and run.

"Sarah . . . you've always been there for me. And I've done all I can to be there for you. I know . . . I know it's not easy living with me. That I don't make enough money. That I'm out at auditions at all hours of the day and night. That I can't—"

She put her tiny finger to his lips and a thrill, a chill, went through him. "Do you remember when we first met?"

"Sure. I asked you to go to the movies with me. Truffaut's *The Four Hundred Blows*."

"And I slapped your face because I thought it was a French porn. We laughed and laughed."

Stan subconsciously rubbed his jaw, as if re-experiencing the pain. "Funny, I don't remember laughing. I vaguely remember looking for a filling . . ."

Sarah knelt down, too, level with the dog, level with Stan, but she wouldn't look at him. "My point is: you taught me so much. About theater, about the arts, about film, about books. You had such potential . . . and . . . I'm trying to stay patient. I'm trying to find the humor in all this. When we first started dating, I would imagine all the amazing things that we would do together. To be honest, meandering in the park watching an unemployed hotdog mascot cleaning up dog shit was not one of them."

Stan rolled up his sleeves, pulled a plastic bag on his hand like an amateur surgeon, happy, for once to have this chore so he could avoid having to respond.

Standing up, looking off into the distance, Sarah closed her impatient eyes. "What do you think about taking a break from acting, just for a bit? Because . . . I need stability. I need to know I have someone I can always rely on. Loyalty, stability . . . that's why I thank God we at least have the dog."

"And . . . what about me? Why do you thank God for me?"

They both tilted their head to a soft sound, just inside the spectrum of human hearing; Sarah put up a single finger as if trying to determine where the sound was coming from. "Is . . . is that your phone?"

"Um, yeah. Yeah, I think it is."

The dog strained and yanked at his taut leash, seeing or smelling something no one else could. Stan clumsily stumbled in his wake, trying, unsuccessfully, to hold him back.

"Could you get it for me?"

She plucked his phone out of his pocket, paced several steps into the distance, while Stan flapped his hands frantically, like an overturned bug. "Quickly please, it could be a job."

"Well, crazier things have happened."

Stan held his breath so long, so hard, he was afraid he would forget how to breathe.

Sarah held the phone out to him. "Someone named Nigel is on the phone for you?"

Stan hurtled over the dog, banged shin-first straight into the corner of a rusty bench, and ripped the phone out of Sarah's surprised hands. "Hi! Nigel, hey there, hello!"

Stan put his hand over the mouthpiece and in his best, raspy stage whisper said to Sarah, "It's Nigel! You know . . . my agent!"

With her left hand, she gave him an enthusiastic thumbs-up while with her right hand, hidden behind her back, she crossed her fingers so firmly that her hand cramped.

"Nigel, wow. I haven't heard from you since . . . well . . . I've . . . I've never heard from you, actually."

Stan took a moment to let this sink in, his posture crumpling several inches, before Nigel spoke again, making Stan's ears perk up momentarily. "Yes . . . oh, my God . . . the cola commercial? . . . Really! . . . What do you mean, 'bring treats'?"

# Chapter 4

The sun rose so slowly that Stan imagined that, just like him, the sun wanted nothing to do with today and just wanted to go back to bed. He had heard of 5:30 AM call times but, having never really been cast in anything before—at least not anything of consequence—he wasn't sure if they truly existed. But here it was. And it was just as awful as he had imagined.

He still couldn't believe it. It had to be a joke. He kept looking around, waiting and praying that any moment now all his friends and relatives would jump out and yell, "Surprise!" and wish him a happy fortieth birthday. Except he was only thirty-three. And his birthday was five and a half months away. As hopes go, it wasn't looking promising.

Looking around, wondering where they were supposed to be, Stan caught sight of the craft services table and fell madly in love. Every hearty baked good, every sun-kissed fruit— lovingly sliced into convenient, bite-size morsels—every flavor of coffee yet thought of by nature or man, was there for the taking, no questions asked. And Stan was sure that if there was a special condiment he desired on the side, that it could be arranged with a whispered word in an influential ear.

With a frolic and a gambol, and a move mildly reminiscent of a caper, he headed for the craft services table, dragging the dog behind him, who had been about to leave a coil-shaped memento, just to prove that he was here. The dog was understandably frustrated at being denied this small opportunity at immortality.

Stan was beginning to regret that he hadn't worn his cargo pants—all those pockets, all those opportunities to hide precious food for later. His lungs panting to try and keep up with the frantic pace, taking great gasps of air in the very small windows of time when there wasn't food in his mouth, Stan's body was about to go into anaphylactic shock. Fortunately for him, though he would never know it to appreciate it, the director was heading straight for him, forcing Stan to stop eating for a moment and frantically brush the mass of crumbs off his fat face.

Stan recognized the intern from the casting session; he was trailing six paces behind the director, keeping his eyes focused on the ground, bowing and scraping in his wake.

As they approached, Stan was rehearsing his greeting to ensure it had the right degree of spontaneity and nonchalance. In his eagerness, Stan offered his hand for a handshake far too early and had to stand there for several excruciating moments like an unused, abandoned hat rack. Not that it mattered, because by the time the director got to him, he completely ignored Stan and bent over to play with the dog.

The director was a hard-looking man, someone who might have been a pirate or an Inquisitor had he been born in another time. He gave off a sense of unpredictable danger, like, if he really had to, if his life really depended on it, or perhaps if he was just a trifle bored, he could rip off your face and then place it on top of his head and then dance around, wearing it like a little hat.

Upon seeing the dog, he acted in a manner somewhat unbecoming to him. "Who's a good doggy woggy, then? Who's my special little guy, huh? My little itty-bitty darling, puppy pooh pooh . . . you cutey wutey, snuggly wuggly chum-chum! Does doggy want a treat? Huh? Who wants a yummy treaty treat?"

Stan was beginning to feel a tad queasy. He had been with Sarah for four years (apparently) and he didn't think he had ever shown her as much affection as the director was showing the dog now, and they had only just met. Stan wasn't sure if he should inquire about the young man's intentions or contact the police.

In mid "coo," the director stood up and was right in Stan's face; in just an instant, he knew the director used a dull shaving blade and apparently enjoyed pickled onions for breakfast. "Who the fuck are you?"

"This . . . well . . . uh . . . you know . . . just . . . I'm . . . I'm with the dog."

With a violent nod of his head in Stan's direction, which was dangerously reminiscent of a professional wrestling head butt, he instructed the intern, "Just make sure that man doesn't shit on my set."

# Chapter 5

Why was it that three o'clock in the morning, if you were still awake and unable to sleep, felt so lonely and friendless? Stan was restless and cold, shivering under what little covers Sarah granted him, his arms and legs askew, as if he had just been thrown from a tall building.

After several agonizing seconds staring at the ceiling, he looked over at her sleeping form beside him. In the faraway glow of the streetlight that leaked through the only apartment window, she looked like the dirty, sexy silhouette of a mud flap girl on the back of an out-of-state freight truck. She was achingly beautiful, curled up, tightly wound, like the wadded-up clump of a spitball. She looked so achingly beautiful, in fact, that Stan felt the need to shove her. Just to be sure she was really asleep. She didn't budge and kept whistling quietly through her nose in perfect tempo; actually, not so quietly: she sounded, snuffled and snorted, like an aging Darth Vader having an asthma attack.

Stan tried again, giving her a slightly harder push—lovingly, of course—but once again, to no avail.

With no other recourse available to him—and goodness knows if there had been another option he would have taken it— he cocked his elbows back, put his clammy palms flat against her curvy back, and tossed her right over the precipice of the bed.

Flailing wildly, Sarah fell the two and a half feet to the floor with a sickening thud; Stan thought, faintly, he heard her mutter some filthy, creative curses. He poked his nose over the edge of the bed, fearful he might have gone too far and timidly asked, "Can't sleep, either, huh?"

Sarah took it all in stride, felt around methodically for broken bones and started the long, slow climb back into bed. "Stan, what's wrong?"

He sat straight up, using ab muscles that would now hurt for at least the next three weeks. "Are you kidding? You know exactly what's wrong. The damn dog, he . . . he . . ."

"But Stan . . . it was just a fluke. Anyway, aren't you proud of him? If you weren't going to get cast anyway, isn't it at least a consolation that your best friend got the part?"

Inching closer to her, leaning back, Stan took her hand. "I've accomplished nothing. Nothing. Do you know what that feels like?"

"Maybe it's time to think about going back to school again? Maybe it's time to rethink why you started acting in the first place?"

"Because I couldn't play guitar, I failed algebra, and I wasn't any good at history, sports, languages, geology, science, or writing."

That wasn't entirely true, if Stan was honest with himself. Not the part about not having any discernible talent in a number of disciplines—that was true enough—but it was only half the story.

"When I'm acting, I know exactly what I'm supposed to say. Well . . . when I remember my lines. I know where I'm going and how I'm supposed to feel when I get there."

And maybe, just maybe, he thought to himself, his early desire to act was a desperate howl for attention from parents who barely knew he was there, whose only ask of their son was that he keep quiet and out of their way. And he had defied them the only way he knew how, the only way a very young Stan could think of: draw as much attention to himself as he could, grab the spotlight, make noise in as public a forum as he could find; in short: act.

If he thought about it a little further, acting had also been his attempt at some degree of immortality, of a neglected child wanting to have some way of proving he was really here, that once, on planet Earth, there briefly lived a man named Stanley Ronald Pavlov who left behind a teeny mark. But that lofty goal was seeming more and more distant with every passing audition.

She moved in closer and Stan held her just a little tighter.

"Sarah . . . if something happened . . . if something ever happened to me . . . I want you to know, I want you to find someone else."

"Okay."

Stan blinked. Sarah yawned.

Stan let out a long breath he didn't even know he was holding. "Well? Isn't there anything you want to say to me?"

"Uh . . . no, I don't think so."

Sarah smiled coyly, tried to give him a soft kiss, but she was clearly too tired to traverse the two-inch chasm between them. They sat there together in the silence for several long moments, until Stan whispered quietly in her ear, "I just . . . I just want to be remembered."

She nuzzled into him so close, so hard, that her bony elbow was prying apart two of his favorite ribs. It hurt like third-world dentistry, but just being this close to her, hearing the lilt in her voice, picturing her name spelled out in longhand . . . looping . . . looping . . . was finally lulling him to sleep.

"Stan, that doesn't matter. There are more important things than just being remembered."

Stan started, yawned, tried again. "Well, my dad always told me, when I was little, the measure of a man is how well he keeps the promises he makes."

"That's nice."

"Of course, he followed that up by telling me to get the fuck out of his face, but still . . ."

Sarah lazily stretched and lay back down, twitched her legs like an old, wet dog. "We're gonna call your parents tomorrow. Let them know we're gonna sue them. Or at least send them invoices for the cost of your therapy."

Mashing his sleepy face with the fat of his hands, Stan mumbled, "No . . . no . . . I don't want to do that. Then I'd have to talk to them."

Stan had confided in Sarah many times before, the complicated relationship with his parents, how lonely his childhood had felt, how he had been primarily raised by the television. It was his babysitter, confidant, and guidance counselor; it had taught him everything he knew about friendship, love, social interaction. It was an awesome responsibility the television had taken on with a tacit complicity.

"Well . . . I suppose your parents only did what they thought was best."

"Sure. But when you think about it, Adolf Hitler only did what he thought was best, so that's a pretty empty defense."

Softly laughing, Sarah's eyelids fell slowly, slowly, slowly. "I never cared about being remembered or about money . . . career . . ."

Her train of thought was interrupted by a wide, hollow yawn. "All I ever really wanted, as long as I can remember, was to meet someone, maybe—"

But Stan was finally asleep.

# Chapter 6

It wasn't just a fluke. Two weeks after the cola commercial aired, the dog started getting offers from every region, in every channel, in every medium, for every genre. He became the biggest thing to hit the Earth since the asteroid that killed off the dinosaurs.

Sarah had given up her regular job (whatever that was) to work solely on taking the dog to and from sets, stages, recording studios. She told Stan one night, after arriving home late from an increasingly common celebrity networking party, she would take over the day-to-day management of the dog so that he could focus on his career. Although, come to think of it, whenever she mentioned his career she did that weird bendy thing with her fingers that Stan never understood, where she made quotation marks in the air. Why was that the only punctuation people mimed? Every time he saw someone do it, he had the urge to flip an exclamation point right back at 'em.

\* \* \*

Nigel had sounded hotly impatient when he called. Impatient and drunk. That wasn't unusual, of course. What was unusual was Nigel wanting to see Stan at all. But, of course, it wasn't Stan he was interested in talking about.

It wasn't much of an office. Nigel didn't have a waiting room. He didn't have a staff. He didn't even have a chair. But Stan could tell from the slur in his voice and the glint in his eye that Nigel felt that was all about to change.

As Stan, dragging the dog behind him, entered Nigel's office quietly, he stepped around something he couldn't identify, then stepped around something he *could* identity and leaned nonchalantly against a dirty corner. Nigel was standing by his desk—or what passed for his desk, it was just a TV tray with cigarette burns scattered at random like miniature moon craters—and jumped up to greet him, arms thrown up high in the air like he was in the last car of a roller-coaster. "Stan! Stan Pavlov! This is the big break we've been waiting for all these years! This is what we've been dreaming about all along! Come on in, my excellent good friends!"

Stan was unnerved by how intently Nigel looked through him.

"You're looking great. Just as I remember you. Did you always not wear glasses?"

Subconsciously, Stan put his hand to the bridge of his nose to double-check before confirming, "Um . . . no. No, I never wore glasses."

Looping his thumbs in his belt loops, and titling his head back, Nigel looked Stan up and down. "You should think about wearing them. Would be a good look for you."

"Well, I have been thinking, maybe—"

"And, how's my good, good boy, huh?" Nigel asked as he got down, level with the dog, and took several slices of turkey out of his worn suit jacket pocket. "Who wants turkey, huh? Who likes the turkey wurkey?"

"Um"—Stan scratched an imaginary itch on the top of his blond head, just for something to do—"you, uh . . . carry turkey slices in your pockets?"

"I do now, yeah."

"Listen, Nigel, while I'm here . . . for the first time . . . ever . . . I was wondering if you think I should update my reel or whether, maybe we should think about—"

Standing up suddenly, Nigel slapped Stan on the back so hard that he staggered as if he had been shot.

"Stan, we're finally gonna make it big! I'm in discussions with the major networks for his own late-night talk show! There's been a few offers for starring roles on Broadway! Musicals, mostly. And the police buddy film scripts are just *pouring* in!"

Nigel's voice softened for a moment, as if he were talking privately to himself. "Just being a small part of the magic . . . that's all I ever asked for . . . and now . . ."

He stopped, bit his lip, as if suddenly aware that he was, in fact, not alone, speaking aloud. In his more comfortable voice, projecting as if he were on the stage himself, he turned back to Stan. "Can you believe it, Stanny Boy? Oh, Stanny Boooooy!"

Holding up a quivering index finger, Stan piped up, "Yeah, you know, I'm really not particularly fond of that nickname."

"Sure you are! You're Irish, aren't ya?"

"No. I'm Russian."

Nigel slipped a battered cigarette in his mouth that he never got around to lighting. "Listen, Stanny Boy, we could sit here all day and argue about what nationality you are, but I'd prefer to tell you what I want from you, pretend I'm busy, and then throw you out of my office. How does that sound?"

"Well, honestly, I—"

*RING!*

"Hang on just a sec . . ."

While Nigel took the call, Stan ran his agitated fingers through his thinning hair. He badly wanted to pace, but Nigel's office was so criminally small he couldn't take more than a few steps in any direction. Frustrated, Stan flopped down on the rugless floor. The dog, never sensing anything was amiss, curled up, snugly, in his lap.

Nigel simply dropped the phone to the floor when he was done, as if checking that gravity was still functioning properly. "That was confirmation he's been cast as the lead in a new prime-time animated series! Next month he's going to have to fly to Los Angeles to record the first episode!"

Stan couldn't believe this. Everything he ever wanted was all happening, it was finally really happening . . . to his dog. He saw his whole career go by in a flash. And then Stan suddenly thought of a way he could make this work. "The dog doesn't actually need to do the voice, does he? I mean, it could be anyone who could do a convincing dog, right? I mean . . . anyone at all . . . even *I* could do the voice. You know?"

Stan cleared his throat; he didn't have time to do his traditional vocal warm-up exercises, time was of the essence. He took three quick, shallow breaths. Showtime. "Woof! Woof woof!"

The phones, the jungle of phones on Nigel's desk, rang again. And again. And again. Nigel held up an astutely manicured finger. "Sorry, excuse me a minute, boys . . ."

Nigel grabbed the phones, one pinched under his cheek, one held to the other ear, cell phones being juggled with whatever digits were left available to him; Stan could tell that with each ring, Nigel saw dollar signs dancing like sugar plums in his head. Undeterred, he continued, "Ah . . . woof! Woof woof!"

Crawling, scampering on the dusty floor, Stan was throwing himself into the role with everything he had.

"Hey! Nigel! Bow wow! Bow wow wow wow wow!"

Nigel tried turning his back on Stan but still couldn't block him out. Trailing in Stan's wake, the dog mimicked each bark, each howl.

"Hello? What? Seriously?"

From the floor, Stan continued his assault from his sore knees. "Hey! Bark! Bark! Arf! Woof!" Putting his hands up in the begging position, he said just a little louder, "I'm . . . I'm barking here, Nigel: a-wooooooooooooooooooooooo!"

"How much? Are you serious?—"

"Nigel, I'm fucking *barking* here!—"

"Hold on, I'll have to check—"

Stan knew it was going to be big news; Nigel's pupils were dilated, which Stan already knew meant: big money.

"It's the Royal Shakespeare Company! They want to know what his range is!"

"What's his range? What's his range?" Stan jumped up off the floor and cocked his leg back, aimed squarely at the dog. "About four feet, that's his fucking range!"

Stan froze, fell into those big, brown eyes he had fallen in love with so long ago. The dog whimpered, cowered, and he wanted to die, wanted to simply melt into the floorboards, for getting this close to crossing an unforgivable line. It was the worst thing he had ever almost done.

Ashamed, but thankful that he had caught himself in time, Stan left and slammed the door. Actually, Nigel's office didn't have a door, just one of those hanging beads things, and Stan was disappointed when it didn't have the effect he had been looking for.

The dog let out a small, sad, whimpering yelp at being left behind.

# Chapter 7

Stan tried to throw himself into his work even though work kept trying to throw him back. He was doing up to five auditions a day and was taking a real method acting approach to each and every one. Before auditioning for the role of *Hamlet* he went out and stabbed an estranged and distant uncle; nothing life threatening, just a graze to get the feel of it. Before auditioning for the titular role in *The Phantom of the Opera*, he spent several nights living and sleeping in the basement of a dusty, dilapidated theater. And the less said about what he did to prepare for a role in *Equus* the better.

Just this morning he had been forcibly escorted off the premises at an audition for a tampon commercial by a small-minded director who didn't have the guts to cast against type. This afternoon, he was foil-deep in a sword fight, auditioning for a musical clusterfuck based on *The Three Musketeers* entitled: *Swashbucklin'!* He had devised a steadfast rule a long time ago that he would never appear in anything where the title ended in an exclamation point. But these were desperate times. To prepare for the role, he had spent all night sleeping in a big, stupid hat and studiously carving his initials in anything and everything with his stage sword. Sarah, understandably, was less than amused.

Clumsily, Stan tied the dog to a rickety stage light, kissed him lightly on his forehead when he was certain that no one was looking, and underwent an elaborate warm-up routine, which involved more arm flailing than Jim Carrey trying to stay upright while sliding across a wide patch of ice.

The audition consisted entirely of a stage combat routine, in which actors were paired off to perform a pre-choreographed sword fight, which, in retrospect, was a bad idea. Actors are so hungry for a part, so utterly desperate for attention, that someone could have easily gotten hurt. And Stan did.

Stan and his auditioning partner danced and pranced around for several minutes, sticking closely with the fight as written: slash, parry, jump, run up a flight of stairs, jump down, lose the sword, dodge a thrust, then run and pick the sword up again, switch hands, parry, thrust, lock swords, lean in and grit teeth at each other—really, just a standard sword fight routine any actor worth his weight in headshots could easily do in his sleep. But as the fight continued, Stan and his partner started showing off, adding little flourishes and jabs, trying to throw each other off of their game. And Stan had held up well. Until one of the casting agents noticed the dog waiting in the wings and asked, "Excuse me, but does your dog know stage combat, too?"

Letting his guard down for just one fatal moment, Stan looked off into the distance and asked, "What?" before he felt the dulled tip of a stage foil press hard against a vital organ he knew he had but didn't think about on a regular basis. And that was when he fainted.

\* \* \*

The hospital bed Stan woke up in was surprisingly comfortable. An annoyingly handsome doctor was standing over him while the nurse probed him in the very few places he would rather she didn't. Although he only had eyes for Sarah, he couldn't help but notice that the nurse was rather attractive in a she-is-definitely-breathing-and-female kind of way, which Stan found irresistible. He could hear the machine monitoring his heartbeat start to overheat and whir as it tried to compensate. Just as he was giving her a new variation of "smile number four"—a little something he had been working on recently—Dr. Fuckwad interrupted and ruined the moment.

"Well, Mr. Pavlov, it was touch-and-go there for a bit, but you've pulled through in the end. You're actually in very good health. There's no reason why you shouldn't live for another thirty or forty years."

Raising an IV-laden arm, in order to share with the doctor a meticulously selected finger, Stan told him, "Fuck you."

With that, the doctor blinked several times in surprise, wrote down a few procedures on Stan's chart that would teach that motherfucker a thing or two, and then calmly sauntered out the door.

As the nurse excused herself and stepped out, Sarah and the dog came bustling in. Both were slightly out of breath and obviously concerned about Stan's well-being. As, indeed, was Stan.

"I came as soon as I heard. How could you do such a thing?"

"Well . . . I really wanted to get the part."

Shading her hand over her eyes, as if she couldn't bear to look at him, she asked, "What the hell are you talking about?"

"Well, occasionally, we actors lie about what we can and can't do in order to get a shot at the audition. Maybe my sword-fighting skills aren't quite what I made them out to be. But the doctor said I'll be fine, just a—"

Sarah stomped her right foot and then did it again, louder, "I'm not talking about your pointless audition, I'm talking about what happened at Nigel's. We just had our weekly financial meeting and he told me all about yesterday."

"Oh . . . oh, that. Nothing to worry about." Stan waved his hand, as if swatting away an imaginary fly. "It will all be fine. We'll swing by Nigel's after they let me out of here and I'll apologize."

Sarah wasn't listening. She was digging through his clothes and his tattered jacket.

"Where are they?"

"Where are what, dear?"

"Keys. Where are your keys?"

Sitting up a little straighter, and grimacing in pain, Stan

pointed to his pile of street clothes curled up on the floor, crumpled as if someone had melted there on the spot. "Oh. They are in the right front pocket of my jeans."

"Great."

"Always put them in the exact same place. Creature of habit, that's me."

"Fine."

Sarah snatched the keys, along with a few lonely bills from Stan's frayed wallet, and headed, shuffled, for the door.

"Wait! Where are you going?"

She gritted her teeth, as if her mouth didn't want her to say what her brain was telling her she should. "I'm leaving. We're through."

"No! Wait! Just . . . wait!"

Sarah paused in the doorway, her slender back still turned to him, her bare shoulders slowly coloring from fair white to embarrassed pink to angry red.

Stan, knowing this was likely his one and only chance, took three quick, shallow breaths. Showtime. "Listen. I know I don't always tell you how I feel, that I keep a lot of things inside. I know I haven't been the best boyfriend—"

She turned and opened her mouth but Stan told her very calmly, "Shut up."

He tightly closed his eyes and continued, "I haven't always been a very good friend. I haven't even always been a very good person. I certainly haven't been a good roommate. I wasn't . . . all right, for the sake of time, let's just say that I haven't been a very good *anything*. If I could go back and relive this time we've had, I would. I would do everything . . . well, better. I would do anything to wake up next to you tomorrow. The only thing besides my dog that ever made me happy was you. I've been so depressed about my career that every day I had to think of a reason to keep going. And that reason was you. And now, lying here, it occurs to me that, after all the time I've spent chasing this dream, there's only one thing I would give it all up for. And that reason is still you. Isn't that worth a second chance?"

"No."

"Jesus! All right, just go, then. But someday—someday soon—you'll realize what you've done, and though we had some problems, we also had something special. And when you realize what a terrible mistake you've made . . . you know what?"

Sarah slowly shook her head, closed her eyes, as if truly surprised Stan was taking this so hard.

"No . . . what?"

"I'll take you back like *that!*"

"Good-bye, Stan."

Momentarily, he thought time stood still, that his optic nerve had hit the pause button on this terrible moment. But then Sarah spoke, rubbing her nose, possibly in anticipation of a mild bout of crying.

"Stan, when is the dog's birthday?"

"May thirteenth."

He could see her grip the dog's leash a little bit tighter, the edge of the leather biting into the fat part of her thin palm, and Stan winced on her behalf.

"Well . . . mine was yesterday."

He was impressed; she had clearly been with him long enough to know a good line to end a scene on. She broke for the door, the dog pulling ahead of her, as if thinking there was nothing more to this exchange between them than finalizing the logistics of a long walk.

Still held prisoner, held down, by the tubes in his arms, Stan fumbled to his knees on the bed. "Wait, wait! You can't take the dog!"

"Yes, I can. And I am. Like I said, Nigel told me what happened in his office. I will not let you near him. You will never see him again."

"But . . . I didn't . . . I didn't do it! I didn't do anything!"

"Listen, Stan . . . I'm sorry. I really am. This isn't going to be easy for any of us. I did love you. I did. I loved the potential of the man I thought you could be. Or would be. But based on what Nigel told me, I'm not letting you anywhere near my dog again."

"But he's *my* dog!"

"No. You're *his* dog. And we both have grown tired of cleaning up your tightly coiled messes."

Stan thought that was the most honest thing Sarah had ever said to him as he felt the metaphorical newspaper of life smack him firmly on the nose.

SEVEN YEARS LATER

# Chapter 8

What was once the old, cramped apartment was now just a collection of echoes, echoes of despair, bare, blank walls of silence that no amount of cluttered, dusty books or cheap, chipped furniture could fill. There was no one left to impress, no one to . . . just no one left. Even now, after all this time, his heart couldn't help but race every time he made the third-to-last stair creak, as if some part of his subconscious was still thinking, just maybe, it was Sarah, coming home.

Week after week, month after month, he just still couldn't believe it; it seemed improbable, impossible that people could continue on, going about their business, as if nothing had happened. How could the whole world not have stopped spinning when his entire life had just fallen apart? Without Sarah, nothing felt right. Sleep was not restful, it was just blacking out. Breathing was no longer an involuntary motion; he had to consciously will his body to keep going. Eating . . . well, eating had never been a problem, he could always eat as much food as was put in front of him, but that wasn't the point. If only she would come back . . .

And then there was the dog. There was no loneliness quite as pronounced, as profound, as a man separated from his dog.

In the intervening years, he had followed his dog's career with interest, buying the DVDs of his movies and wishing his dog well the way you wish well an old girlfriend who ripped your heart right out of your chest and stepped on it—through gritted teeth and with zero sincerity. The dog's success had lasted about three, maybe four, years before it dissolved as quickly as it had all started.

Finding a new dog would have been as easy as could be, just a stroll down to the rescue center. Finding a new girlfriend was proving to be far more of a challenge. It wasn't easy to accept that maybe, quite likely, he was going to just be on his own from now on.

But eventually, finally, he accepted it.

Just as he had accepted that he had been very late to find adulthood; he had waited until quite late in life to give up on his childhood dream. He couldn't even remember which audition it had been, what role it was for; what he did remember was that empty-feeling epiphany he had in mid-sentence, realizing the absurdity of the situation, the pointlessness of pretending to be someone else. He simply walked off the stage.

He had given the corporate grind an honest try—all those little offices, with their glass doors and conference rooms, as if it were a human zoo. The transparency of the work space was, of course, intended to feel freeing, like it was an open and breathable space, but it was really just cruelty; cruel because it made them fully aware that there was in fact a world outside and that it was passing them by. He realized that he needed to at least be around the stage, if he couldn't actually be on it.

Without thinking about it, just aimlessly wandering the streets one day, he inexplicably found himself in front of the Reflex Players Theater and he ambled inside with his hat, metaphorically, in his humble hands. The director Stan had initially worked for had moved on to bigger and better things; he'd died.

But he found that the new director was kind; he gave Stan a chance and a menial, thankless job, doing unspecified tasks no one else wanted.

Tonight, the stage was bare, barring a few scattered well-worn chairs, a few scattered well-worn actors, but Stan could see a whole world unfold; he could truly believe that there was a grand courtroom right there in front of him, peopled by lords and cardinals, the scene brought more and more to life with each passing word. There were times—many times if he were honest—where he suddenly found himself mouthing along with the words; he simply couldn't help himself.

How beautiful language could sound, when articulated by the right person, in the right way, the sounds rolling around the mouth, how it changed as it interacted with teeth, tongue, lips . . .

Most of the actors just flat-out ignored him, which was just fine by Stan. Applause, attention, the promise of fame—these no longer held any allure. All he wanted, needed, was the occasional pat on the head.

The company was just two weeks away from opening night of their latest modern adaptation of Shakespeare: *Henry VIII: The Revenge.* Stan was afraid they might have missed the point of the play, but what the hell did he know? His was not to question why; his was but to do and clean up afterward.

They were in the middle of rehearsing the trial scene and Stan found himself completely riveted. He was reminded of what had drawn him to the profession in the first place; he was able to be transposed, to be completely entranced and taken to another time, another place.

"What the *fuck* are you doing?"

Even without his cape, his costume, the actor playing King Henry was imposing, commanding. He stood, hands on hips, as if demanding an answer from his subject. The cast froze in tableau. When the painful silence continued, Stan put his hands up, as if he were the helpless victim in a hostage negotiation, and squeaked, "Um . . . nothing. Nothing. I'm . . . sorry."

Pointing an accusing finger, as if it were Stan on trial, King Henry projected, "Don't be sorry—*think* for one fucking second! You're whispering the lines as I'm trying to perform here and, hey, it's fucking *distracting.*"

Damn. He'd been mouthing the words out loud again. He shoved his hands in his pockets and gripped the spare fabric within an inch of its inanimate life. "Yeah. Yeah . . . I'm . . . sorry . . . I'm just—"

King Henry, without looking, viciously kicked over a stage light, which wobbled, tipped slowly, and cracked onto the floor, like a giant, felled redwood. "Do you understand my mind is not in the scene if you're doing that? For fuck's sake, you're amateur."

Fighting to keep his bottom lip from quivering, Stan softly backed up, as if hoping he could just dissolve into the background and disappear.

"Just wait in the wings where you belong and stay off the fucking stage. You're a nice guy, but you and I are done professionally. Hey—doesn't anyone have something to say to this prick?"

The director nobly stepped up to come to Stan's defense when no one else did. "Okay, okay. Relax. Let's just take a minute."

As if he were ordering Stan's beheading, King Henry puffed himself up, nearly jumped out of his skin and with a wild sweep of his arm shouted, "No! Let's not take a minute! Get this prick off the stage and then let's go again!"

\* \* \*

The director's office hadn't changed much apart from the furniture, the decor, the layout, and the location. It seemed like an inappropriate percentage of Stan's life was spent being hauled across the carpet of some authority figure's office. He didn't deliberately rebel against authority, he just could never figure out how to fit in the way he was expected to fit in.

The new director sat behind his desk holding a nonchalant glass of iced tea as if he were posing for a print ad. His posture was so rigid, so straight, Stan's back started to hurt on his behalf. The director held out his hands, Buddha-like, hovering above his desk as if he were holding up an imaginary shelf. "Stan, I'm sorry about what happened, I really am. But you know as well as I do what actors can be like. But I have no intention of firing you. You're dependable. Loyal. You cost us practically nothing and you're completely harmless. Besides, it isn't easy to find someone who doesn't mind rolling up his sleeves and cleaning up other people's messes."

Stan looked the director in the eye, nodded slightly, even smiled. "Good. Thank you. That's very good to hear. And I appreciate it. Because . . . because . . . I quit."

If the director was surprised by this, he wasn't half as surprised as Stan was. Stan blinked several times, rapidly, rubbed his eyes as if someone had thrown cold water on him. He hadn't planned on saying that but for once, his gut overrode his brain, his ego got the better of his reason.

Stan gave the director a firm handshake, a wan smile, a wave, and let himself out.

# Chapter 9

Stan had frequented the same dank, dark bar across the street from the theater nearly every night, but he knew tonight would be the last time he would ever visit; he didn't want to bump into anyone he knew. His pride in having taken the high ground was slowly giving way to the embarrassment of what happened, not to mention that he wanted to avoid the dreaded question: "So what are you going to do now?"

He had tried following his dream, he had tried settling; neither worked. What would he do now?

He was making one last all-out attempt to make something of the night. He had been trying to chat up a young brunette for the last ten minutes. She was so covered in jewelry, he imagined that when she opened her jacket, there was a menagerie of wrist-watches that she sold in dark alleys and off the back of dirty, unmarked white vans. After the third drink she "accidentally" spilled (in his face), she lost the last vestige of her patience. "Listen, you seem very . . . well . . . I'm sure you have some good quality . . . hidden under there . . . somewhere . . . but I'm really not interested—"

"But—"

She held up a hand, as if directing traffic. "And I just broke off a five-year relationship and I'm just not looking to be with anyone right now."

"Yeah, well, I don't believe in that idea that when you break up you need to have time and space."

Stan flashed her "smile number four"—now that he had the move rehearsed and perfected—and gently put his hand on her arm, which she must have mistaken for a more aggressive move, for she slapped him, hard, across the face, the jangling bangles clattering on her arm and making a surprising amount of noise.

She briskly walked away to sit at another table; as she left,

Stan tried one last attempt. "Hey, baby, I can teach you things . . . I can teach you things you didn't even want to *know*!"

Okay . . . a lot of people saw that. No matter. Stan knew, from many years of experience, you could miss a line, drop a prop, accidently trip and fall flat on your face, but if your next scene went well, the audience never remembered the earlier mistake. He strode up to the bar and squeezed himself between two women who did everything they could to make him unwelcome. They crowded the space in between them so thoroughly that Stan made a physical noise as he pried them apart to belly up to the bar. He turned to the woman to his left but before he could open his mouth, she declared, "Recent lesbian."

Undeterred, Stan turned to the woman on his right, who, without looking at him, said loudly, "*Very* recent lesbian."

Stan waved down the bartender. "Excuse me, is this a lesbian bar?"

"It is since you walked in."

Stan let his heavy head fall forward, noting that the bar was riddled, sloppily carved, with such obscene graffiti it would have made Andrew Dice Clay blush.

The bartender, scrupulously wiping a glass with a foul rag that was making the glass far dirtier than it had even been, gave Stan a fatherly slap on the arm. "Hey . . . maybe it's just not your night, huh?"

"No . . . no . . . this my usual luck. You know, I was once rejected five times in less than fifteen minutes."

Nodding, the bartender leaned on the bar, his chubby forearms getting stuck to something Stan didn't really want to think about. "Yeah, I've heard speed dating can be rough."

"What's speed dating?"

He didn't notice the bartender slink quietly backwards into the shadows because out of the corner of his bleary eye, Stan couldn't believe what he had just seen. Or, more accurately, *whom* he had just seen, heading his way, flagging him down. At first, he put it down to the stress of the day, that his brain was conjuring up images from his past, as if in a dream. Then he remembered that he didn't care about losing his job and that he wasn't the slightest bit stressed. He decided the visage was real enough to react to.

Stan shuffled forward, painfully, like an eighth-grade boy at a school dance. "Nigel? What . . . what are you doing here?"

"Me? What about you? I couldn't believe it when the guys at the Reflex Players Theater told me you were here."

"Well, I've fallen on some hard times and this place doesn't judge—"

Nigel popped a stubby, half-used, unlit cigarette in his mouth. "No, I don't mean at this dive bar, I mean on this planet. I figured you would have starved to death a long time ago."

"Now, look here—"

*RING!*

"Sorry, hold on one second—"

Stan's resentment had to quietly fester and stew while Nigel flipped open his phone and had, what sounded like, depraved, degraded phone sex. To Stan, whose indignation eventually found a quiet place in his heart to nuzzle up against, fizzle, and die, it sounded quite painful.

When Nigel hung up he turned to Stan and continued, without missing a beat, as if he had just been checking in on his elderly mother, "So, anyway . . . I'm glad I finally found you. I've been trying to get ahold of you all week. Believe it or not, I may have a job for you. A real, honest-to-God acting job!"

Stan backed away, slowly at first, then with increasing urgency until he backed straight into the wall.

"No, no. I don't act anymore."

As he spoke, Nigel smoothed his thinning hair in the glass reflection just behind Stan. "Really? But you were so dedicated?"

Stan couldn't look at Nigel, couldn't look at anything. "Yeah, well, sometimes no matter how badly you want something, it just doesn't want you back."

Nigel put his hand on Stan's shoulder, but lightly, as if he were afraid of getting his fingers dirty. "Listen, how long have we known each other?"

"A long goddamn time."

"A long goddamn time, that's right. And wouldn't you say we've become pretty close, Ted?"

"Stan."

"Whatever. Listen. I have a job for you. I'm talking about a serious lead here. Network television. Prime time. Hosting your very own game show."

"No."

Nigel punched, mashed, a fist into his hand; Stan didn't think people really did things like that. "What's the problem? Are you too good to work on a game show? Look where integrity has gotten you so far . . . absolutely nowhere, that's where." Nigel dug his finger into Stan's collarbone, making him wince. "I could buy and sell you."

Blood rushed to Stan's face, amplifying the torrid pulsing in his ears. He effeminately slapped Nigel's hand away, momentarily forgetting his years of stage fight training. "I'm . . . I'm not for sale, Nigel."

"Oh, yes. Yes, you are. Everyone is. You just don't know at what price yet."

Stan turned to walk away, but Nigel grabbed the coarse fabric of his sleeve, squeezed a lot harder than Stan thought him capable of. "Listen . . . I don't have the courage to get up in front of people. I never have. But I've always admired . . . envied . . . those who can. When my clients get applause . . . I feel . . . I feel like I'm getting just a little of that applause, too. The attention. The respect. Please . . . just come to one dinner meeting with some TV execs I've been working with. Just hear 'em out."

Dinner? Free dinner? In a deep, distant corner of his mind, Stan heard the shrill sound of three distinct rings . . .

# Chapter 10

Stan showed up at the restaurant late, drunk, and prepared to eat himself stupid. As a concession, he had agreed, among himself, to wear a stifling and stuffy blue-collared shirt, but he left it untucked and absolutely refused to don a tie; and when realization hit that his buttons were askew and misaligned, he outright declined to do another take and left it, giving him a slightly humpbacked, pirate-like look.

He dreaded meetings like these. He made a conscious, deliberate point of not learning the names of the executives he was here to meet: two greasy, dead-eyed vampires, about as warm as Chicago sleet, as appealing as tire-tracked road kill, as reassuring as the legal disclaimer at the end of a pharmaceutical ad. They mirrored each other's movements grotesquely, one usually lagging just a few seconds behind the other, as if they were connected by invisible thread. One of them had hair so coiffed it looked like it was made out of Styrofoam and the other one was outrageously bald, but thought three pathetic hairs combed over his bumpy, naked skull would fool the rest of civilization. In his head, Stan dubbed them Blow Dry and Comb Over.

They wore identical business blue suits and interchangeable crisp, lightly starched, white shirts; they both wore red-striped ties but, in a bold stroke of individuality, they were just slightly different shades. And they never stopped smiling. Even while they were eating. That seemed physically impossible, but there they were, right in front of Stan's disbelieving eyes.

Nigel sat perched on the edge of his seat, as if he might go for any of their throats at any moment, teeth grinding quietly on the ice from his water glass.

During the appetizer course, Stan ate so much shrimp he could feel it filling his sinus cavity. During dinner, he ordered three meals. One he shoveled down his throat, one he folded up and tucked neatly in his pants and one he simply dumped on the floor to illustrate his contempt. It was during the dessert course that Comb Over finally got down to business. "We gotta tell you, Stan, we think we've really got something here."

Blow Dry, with his manicured fingers held up high as if he were modeling hand cream, added, "Something big."

"Something fresh—"

"Something hot—"

"You sound like an excerpt from *Letters to Penthouse*," Stan offered.

Nigel crunched noisily on the ice from his water glass.

Comb Over turned to Blow Dry and Blow Dry turned to Comb Over. For the briefest of moments it looked as if their smiles might falter. But style, locked in its eternal war with substance, won yet another battle.

They turned back to face Stan, smiles firmly etched into their faces. Stan could actually see their back molars. It was like having dinner with The Joker and the most recent winner of the Miss America pageant. It would have been enough to put most people off their food. But not Stan, who was now reaching over to adjacent tables and taking whatever food he could grab before they started striking him.

Nigel huffed and sighed, peering deeply into his water glass, clearly wishing he had more ice.

Blow Dry carefully, lovingly, caressed his coif, as if what he dared to call hair could possibly be out of place. "Okay, Stanny Boy, let's put all the cards on the table."

Stan shook his head, closed his eyes. "Yeah, you see, I'm not really particularly fond—"

"We are getting killed on Wednesday nights," Comb Over confessed.

"We are up against that reality show," Blow Dry whispered, picking up the thread of the story now in hushed tones. "You know, the one where people eat disgusting things, betray their friends and family, fall down and severely hurt themselves, get randomly hit in the crotch with flying objects. You know the kind of thing. Disgusting stuff."

"And on the other network," Comb Over seamlessly jumped in, "we are up against that show where people send in home videos of people eating disgusting things, betraying their friends and family, falling down and severely hurting themselves, and getting randomly hit in the crotch with flying objects."

"It's really quite funny," Blow Dry chimed in and let out a long laugh that sounded like a man gasping for air after being resuscitated from drowning. Stan wasn't sure if they should join in or perform CPR. Thankfully, he eventually stopped without any obvious injury to himself.

"Last week Nigel shared with us your reel and a few of your old audition tapes. You really caught our interest."

Stan, surprised at this development, wanted to say something meaningful but could only articulate a half-hearted: "Huh?"

They simply ignored him, continued the gist of the discussion.

"We"—and here Blow Dry and Comb Over looked at each other conspiratorially— "have developed a game show formula for the everyday schlub."

"And," Comb Over jumped in, "we need an everyday schlub to *host* it."

"Stan"—and here Blow Dry reached across the table and put his hand on top of Stan's, which was an oddly human gesture for a man who was so cold, Stan would not have been surprised if he had not had a pulse—"listen to me . . . are ya listening? We want someone the audience can identify with."

"Yeah, someone who isn't, you know, good-looking or particularly smart," Blow Dry chimed in.

"Right! Someone who . . ." Comb Over stumbled, waved his hands in the air as if wafting away smoke, as he struggled to find the words. Or maybe he was choking on a chicken bone. Stan didn't care either way. "Someone who . . . gives off an air of failure."

"Of self-loathing."

"Remorse!"

"A real fuckwad!"

"A sad, pathetic schnook without any . . . you know . . . redeeming value to the evolution of the human species."

"And we think you'd be *perfect*."

An unsteady whiskey glass trembled, shuddered, slightly in Stan's hand. Stan thought it humane to put it out of its misery and so he drained the glass with what little coordination remained in him. For several moments, they all stared quietly at each other like in an old-fashioned Western Stan had once auditioned for and didn't get.

Stan knew he would never get another chance like this.

"Guys, I want to thank you for the offer. Really. I fully appreciate that, for me, this is probably the offer of a lifetime."

Comb Over and Blow Dry exchanged contented smiles with themselves and then with Nigel.

With one hand steadying himself on the table and with one hand filling his pockets with more shrimp and with one hand slicking back the cowlick in his hair (how was he doing that? Even Stan was surprised; he must be drunker than he'd thought), he stood up from the table.

"And I mean it when I say you can both fuck your grandmothers in the ear with an overripe banana. You manipulative, lice-ridden, inbred cuntmuppets."

Still smiling. The sons of goddamn bitches were still goddamn smiling.

"Just think about it, Stan," wheezed Comb Over.

"Yeah, that's all we ask," Blow Dry added, his voice dripping with the temptation of forbidden fruit. "You don't have to make a decision right now. Just kick the idea around a little. Sleep on it."

# Chapter 11

It was a chilly, gray-skied, no-moon night; the heat of the day—the fetid, stale air—was still trapped under the canopy, the smoky rooftop, of a sizzling, smoky haze. Stan staggered toward home—at least he hoped it was toward home—with a blinding, blurry headache. He was not pleased with how the evening had gone. How dare the powerful and influential offer jobs out of the blue to poor, desperate, pathetic nobodies? It made him sick. Well, sicker than he already was. He paused momentarily to throw up in a passing mailbox as he contemplated the eternal mysteries of life.

All in all, though, he did have one reason to be pleased with himself: that for once he wouldn't do anything for a part; how he had survived the last temptation. Maybe this was the final stand he needed to officially confirm that, at long last, he had found the cure for the acting bug; maybe it was—with all of its anxiety, insecurity, uncertainty—now truly out of his system for good.

Stan watched the stars ever so slowly turn as he made his way home. His ringing phone, three quick, successive rings, startled him and then made him angry . . . damn Nigel . . . calling him to try and talk him into selling out even after all that . . .

Stan checked his phone. *Oh, my God, it's Sarah. Sarah!* How many times should he let it ring before answering in order to give off the right degree of insouciance? Three? Five? Let it go straight to voice mail?

He picked it up before the first ring ended, cradling the phone as if he were, at last, holding her again. "Sarah?"

Damn. He'd spoken too fast. Too high-pitched. Too desperate. Too "if you came back now I'd spend all night with you listening to Journey's *Escape* while taking a bubble bath and shit."

"Before you start, let me just clarify that this isn't a social call. I'm calling about the dog."

Stan put his hand up to stop her right there, forgetting, momentarily, she couldn't see him. "Wait, wait. After all these years you really don't have anything else to talk to me about?"

"Fine, if you would like me to humor you momentarily with small talk, I will."

"Great."

There was an awkward pause, so silent and profound, that Stan thought he could hear the Earth, clinging tightly to its imaginary axis, turn ever so slowly against the black vastness of space.

"So . . . how are you?"

"Okay."

"Happy?"

"Not really."

"Still acting?"

"No."

There followed another long pause, which Stan filled with such disgusting and depraved fantasies about Sarah that it would have embarrassed Caligula.

Stan knew this was his only chance to reconcile. He should tell her. Tell her everything she meant to him. How hollow life felt without her, how the universe seemed a cold, godless, barren void without her by his side. She was a burning, bright star and he was but a humble, rocky planetoid, inexorably drawn to her, needing her to soundlessly illustrate to him an unwavering path to happiness, to truth. "Listen, do you wanna meet up for a quickie?"

"Are you physically capable of any other way?"

He shook his head, laughed long and silently. "Sometimes I forget which one of us had the improv training."

In the brief silence, he closed his eyes tight, shutting out everything else, as if he and Sarah were the only two people in the entire world. She broke his meditation. "So . . . uh . . . do you have a new dog?"

Sitting down on someone's random front steps, Stan stretched out his legs and leaned back to look up into the endless night sky, imagining he was looking deeply into Sarah's face one more time. "I did eventually get a new dog, for a little while, yeah. Had to be sure he had no acting aspirations. This dog was as dumb as a plank. Just like everyone else, he eventually ran away and left me. Had to teach him everything. Even how to lick his balls."

"He didn't know how to do that?"

"Well . . . it never hurts to brush up on the basics."

"For you or him?"

Stan stood up too fast, wobbled, "Wait, what—"

"Listen, I really don't have time for this, Stanny Boy . . ."

Stan placed his free hand over his bloodshot eyes, as if he were playing hide-and-seek. "Yeah, you see, I'm not really particularly fond of—"

"I have to talk to you about your dog."

"Oh, so now he's *my* dog . . ."

"Stan . . . listen . . ."

# Chapter 12

The worst part was the lights. Funny, that after all those years onstage—from the kindergarten Christmas pageant (he played a duck about to be beheaded for Christmas dinner) to his final performance with the Reflex Players Ensemble (a desk)—that the lights should prove to be so troublesome.

Perhaps it felt so self-indulgent after feeling so forgettable for so long. Perhaps it was how many people—surly, lazy, angry, sometimes completely stoned people, but people nonetheless—it took to get all that electrical equipment focused on him. Or perhaps, somewhere deep in his subconscious, it felt as if the lights metaphorically exposed all the poor choices, all the mistakes, all the darkness in his heart, all the frustrations that led him to where he was now, at this awful and disgraceful moment in time.

Or perhaps the lights just made him a bit sweaty.

But in the end, if he were honest with himself, it wasn't nearly as hard to defecate on his values as he had been led to believe.

All that money. The dog had blown all that money in just seven years. According to Sarah, he had blown it all on chew toys. And bitches. Huh. How many times had Stan been down that road?

Twenty thousand dollars. Twenty. *Thousand.* Dollars. That's how much the dog's operation was going to cost. It seemed like an excessive amount. If it had been for one of his parents, he would have said, sorry, no, it's been a nice run, but in the end everyone has their time and everyone dies. If it had been for Sarah, he would have acquiesced, but it would have resulted in some long, sleepless nights. But for the dog, for that damn dog, there was no question. He would do whatever needed to be done—even become the host of a game show.

He had reluctantly moved to Los Angeles, with nothing more

than a small and half-empty suitcase and a table lamp, knowing that he not only couldn't afford a three-thousand-mile commute but that if he was going to really go through with this, he would have to take the leap and fully act the part.

It wasn't that he didn't like Los Angeles; it was just that it was so different from New York. It was hard to believe these two cities could be part of the same planet, let alone part of the same country. New York had an air of possibility, of opportunity. Los Angeles always felt unstable to Stan—and not just because the ground sometimes moved under his feet. It was like you could be so many different people here, even from one day to the next. While Stan was sure that felt freeing to some people, it just made him queasy. It was like he was afraid he would go to bed a butterfly and wake up a caterpillar.

New York felt like a lifetime ago but it had only been about a month since he first went on-air. He was already getting frequently stopped in public. People would cross the street just to ask him, "Hey, aren't you the host of *Animal Instinct*?" Or they would recite back to him his already tiresome catchphrase: "Get up, come on down, and roll over!" Or they would grab him by the sleeve and ask, "Hey, how the hell do I get to Andover Street?"

He had to confess those bastards, Comb Over and Blow Dry, had been right: this was the part he was born to play. Not exactly Everyman, more like . . . Nothingman.

The more ordinary he came across, the more the audience adored him. They identified with him. He had once been just like them—nothing—but then he had just a little stroke of luck and was now doing exceptionally well, and it inspired them to see one of their own catch a break. He was just like the rest of the crowd, having once had dreams and ambitions, an overwhelming desire to leave just a little mark behind when they shuffled off this mortal coil, knowing that someday we would all just be dust, but now, like them, he just wanted to be entertained, to be given something for nothing, like a free appliance, and take the occasional nap.

Upon hearing the first note of the theme song, the inane insect-like chatter turned instantly into the hushed awe of the Church of Materialism. Stan could see some of them salivating in anticipation of getting The Finger.

He had not planned on it being a signature move or anything of consequence, but it was already being imitated and parodied in more places than he could name. Before selecting that night's contestants, Stan would hold up his index finger and wave it back and forth in anticipation, like some inbred Roman emperor declaring whether the performers would or would not get fed to the lions. After several agonizing moments, Stan would suddenly—*BANG!*—point out a member of the audience, who would jump up and down, knowing their lives would be changed forever. Even if they won nothing but a copy of the home game— and who the hell was so bereft of ways to entertain themselves that they played the home game?—they would be able to say, long into their dotage, that they had once appeared on TV.

As the theme song came to its conclusion, Stan saw the son of a bitch in the booth—who took home a real paycheck, payable in legit U.S. currency, for saying one damn sentence a *week*—clear his throat and prepare to bellow into the microphone. He didn't even have the originality to come up with a unique, signature cadence, he just elongated the vowels like every other game show and talk show announcer of the last forty years. Stan had never even met him but hated him with a deep, fiery, passionate disgust for everything he stood for. "And now, heeeeeeeeeeere's your host of *Animal Instinct*, Stanny Booooooooooy!"

Stan opened his mouth to object and then remembered the producers had let it leak that this was his preferred nickname, thinking it added to his regular-guy mystique. It had caught on so quickly that by the third episode the contestants and the announcer referred to him as nothing else, thinking it was warm and chummy, while instead Stan felt ill with every utterance.

His lily-white silk shirt was itchy and didn't fit right; he pulled and stretched the fabric one last time before heading out onstage. Nigel had convinced him to wear thick-rimmed, black-framed glasses with false lenses in them, even though Stan's eyesight was perfect; Nigel thought it would make Stan look a little older, approachable, a better fit for the part. Stan wiggled the frames back to a more comfortable place and glared out into the crowd . . .

At every recording they received a useless little goody bag courtesy of one of the sponsors, which he saw they all had clutched in their sweaty little hands, like small children collecting their favors at a birthday party. Each time the goody bags were handed out, with about thirty cents' worth of trinkets—things like sample sizes of hand lotion, travel-size toothpaste, pocket facial tissues—they hooted and hollered like they would never have to work again in their lives. Stan realized if they had been given a free bag full of rhinoceros dung they still would have whooped it up, just because it was free, just because it felt like they had been just that little bit luckier than everyone else.

Comb Over and Blow Dry had given him the secret formula that, Stan had to admit, was working. Of the three contestants he was to select, one should always be a hot MILF. Another, should be a feisty older person who didn't have any dignity and acted thirty years younger than they were (male/female optional). The third could be a wild card, though with the caveat that two out of every five concurrent wild card selections (non-inclusive of holidays, weekends, and programing interruptions for stupid shit like breaking news, the Olympics, or the president), needed to be representative of diversity, though gender selection was still allowed to be up to Stan's discretion.

The stagehand across the way gave Stan his visual cue, indicating there were five seconds until he was on; Stan jogged out, stepped on his mark and took three quick, shallow breaths. Showtime.

It was the television game show host's curse that he had to repeat the same lines over and over and over . . . like starring in a long-running play, it was an actor's responsibility to make it feel—or at least sound—fresh. He rotated toward the mesmeric lure of the camera, hypnotizing him with its one unblinking, unfaltering eye, which sucked him in; he could feel its inescapable pull, as if he were being physically transported through to the other side . . .

"Welcome to—"

"*Animal Instinct!*" the crowd roared.

Stan dramatically got into a semi-crouch. "The show where you have to—"

"*Walk like an animal!*"

He then moved his left hand, as if maneuvering an invisible puppet. "And you have to —"

"*Talk like an animal!*"

The crowd was really responding; they were picking up their cues faster and faster with each episode. Stan couldn't believe they said half his lines for him now, but he still got paid the full amount; it was the perfect gig for a man who wasn't so good on learning his lines.

"And you have to—" And here Stan made a cartoony frowny face while putting his index finger to his head.

"*Think like an animal!*"

Finally, Stan mimed drinking water from a bowl. "And you have to—"

"*Drink like an animal!*"

They were foaming at the mouth now. So happy to have a place, to know what was expected of them, to have no stress or demands put on them. They could just . . . forget. It was clear to him that they would follow him into battle right now if he asked them to. They would march right off the edge of the Brooklyn Bridge. They would do anything to be part of the magic. Sadly, he had no better plan, no place to lead them.

"So—"

And here the audience was shouting right along with him . . . *"Get up, come on down, and roooooooll over!"*

The premise of the game was simple: three specially selected jackasses came up onstage and had to act like different animals performing particular behaviors or actions. Then a panel of semi-celebrities—if you could count the spokesman from a paper towel commercial or the latest manufactured, androgynous train wreck from an Andrew Lloyd Webber musical fiasco a semi-celebrity—had to guess what they were doing. Apparently, there were no points for guessing "humiliating themselves and dishonoring their ancestors," probably as it was just too obvious. Stan knew; he had checked with the judges.

As the first contestants climbed up onstage, Stan vaguely wondered if, a hundred years from now, rather than studying Dickens or Shakespeare, schools would screen soap operas and game shows as twenty-first-century "classics" and some somber middle school kids would have to write a paper on his performance. Was this how his century would be remembered?

Before he knew it, the show was over, and he started heading toward the silent sanctuary of his dressing room, where another nameless, faceless assistant was handing him a towel, a drink, and a smorgasbord of drugs—which he politely refused. The episode was out there now, another serving of empty entertainment calories.

Nigel was waiting for Stan in front of his dressing room door, like he had been at the end of every single recording.

Stan let out a groan, couldn't be bothered to try and disguise it. "Nigel, I assumed that after the first few weeks you'd stop hanging around backstage. That you'd know I have it all under control."

"Well, you know what they say happens when you assume, don't you? That you make an ass out of *U* and *me*."

"Yeah, well, you're half-right," Stan mumbled.

"Sorry, what?"

Utilizing all the body language he knew, he tried to give Nigel every possible non-verbal signal that he had no interest in talking further. He leaned left, then went right, like a boxer warming up. When Nigel failed to react, Stan tried another tack. "Listen, I appreciate all you're trying to do. I appreciate that you're trying to be helpful. But you don't need to be here. I'm better . . . alone. It's really best when I'm alone. Now, excuse me . . ."

Reaching for the doorknob, as if it were the break tape at the end of a painful marathon run, Stan tried to push Nigel aside, slightly more roughly than was socially acceptable, but Nigel didn't move.

"Listen, Stan, I came out west with you so I could take care of you, to be sure you have everything you need. And . . . maybe it's also my way . . . my small way . . . of making up for all the years that I failed you."

Nigel toyed with an open box of cigarettes, rubbing his fingertips delicately over each one, as if it were a musical instrument, gazing deeply into the carton, as if what he really wanted to say was written down for him inside. "This is just the start. We're going on quite a journey, you and me. We're going to be embarking on this adventure . . . together . . . my . . ." And here, as if it was the very first time he had ever used the word and was afraid he would pronounce it wrong, he added, ". . . friend."

Stan was too tired to smile politely; he simply rubbed his forehead, felt the clumpy stage makeup come away in his hands. "Well, I hope you didn't give up your old apartment. I won't be doing this much longer."

"Well, anyway . . . I'm glad you didn't end up quitting after that first paycheck after all. What made you change your mind?"

Stan's eyes chose to betray him. He looked around guiltily before his eyes crashed straight into the slender visage of his co-host suspiciously loitering in the doorway of her dressing room down the hall. She was just one more piece of the master plan by

Comb Over and Blow Dry to establish a stranglehold on Wednesday night television viewing for years to come.

Stan let his eyes linger and take a long, longing look at her, at Mary Schrödinger—"Ms. Schrödinger to you,"—he remembered her telling him, flirtatiously, and thought, for a game show co-host, she wasn't really that attractive. Unless you're attracted to a woman who is a slinky, leggy, peroxide blond. Which he was.

She caught him looking at her and she gave him such an innuendo-laden wink that his legs turned to warm, orange marmalade. He quickly looked down at the floor and silently prayed that when he looked up again she would be looking somewhere else.

He looked up. She wasn't looking somewhere else. *Thanks a lot, God. Thanks for nothing.*

He wanted her so badly, he had devised a fiendishly clever plan: any time she came near him he'd run like fuck. That should work.

To his astonishment, she had already tried coming on to him. Stan was so nervous he had nearly wet his pants. It had been so unbelievably long since he had been with a woman he was afraid he had forgotten what was supposed to go where and he would just end up either hurting or impregnating himself.

Mary, that walking temptation, strode over and took their attention, and their breath, away. Nigel excused himself, sauntered off; he declared that he had some new sly publicity scheme to attend to, and Stan apparently had a conversation with Mary, nodding and smiling. But if someone had asked him, he would have had no recollection of what she had said and just hoped he wouldn't be agreeing to anything too incriminating.

Eventually, his neck was sore from continuously bobbing like fishing tackle at the feet of a sleeping fisherman, and he realized, to his horror, she had said something to which a nod and a smile had been an illogical response. He thought maybe he should try talking. How hard could it be, right? He vaguely did that for living, didn't he?

Leaning back against his doorframe, he tried to cross his arms, casually, and somehow, inexplicably, missed. "Mah gunnah fffnnnmpf nghaga deedledooh." Damn.

"Um . . . I'm sorry?"

*Come on, man! Pull yourself together. You can do this. Breathe.*

Forcing himself to look at her, he was unnerved when he spoke, how his voice didn't sound like the voice he had lived with his whole life; he tried several different pitches, until he found the one that sounded the most familiar. "Sorry. Sorry about that. It's my accent. Most Americans can't understand what I'm saying unless I really concentrate."

"Oh? Where are you from originally?"

"Boston."

"Oh."

Stan looked at his shoes, noting that he had never had such shiny, stiff, confining footwear in his life; they were stifling. All he wanted was to get out of them, get out of here, get out of this place . . .

Mary suddenly put her hand on top of his and he willed himself to not sweat, to not shake.

"Look . . . Mr. Pavlov . . ." She lowered her eyes, then reconnected. "Stan. There's something I've been wanting to discuss with you. . . ."

# Chapter 13

Stan had agreed to come to Mary's apartment under some poorly articulated pretense regarding the show, but it had been so feeble, he had completely forgotten what it was. And although he was certain any involvement with a coworker was a bad idea, he couldn't help but be utterly captivated by her. Not really for who she was, but for what she represented: the type of dangerously attractive woman who, before he had become famous, would have been more likely to slam a broken beer bottle in his face than give him the time of day.

He felt nervous, apprehensive, but truly alive, that feeling you have after nearly being crushed by the big tractor-trailer truck that unexpectedly comes crashing into your lane, when you can feel the blood pumping in your veins, the electrical pulses firing in your brain stem, and a faint but persistent wave of nausea.

He knew she greeted him at the front door, but that's about all he was sure of, he had no idea what, if anything, she had said, as a heavy fog wrapped itself around him and smothered all conscious and logical thought. It was far easier to look around at her apartment than to look at her. Her apartment was a lot like Mary herself: small, tasteful, boldly decorated. As he entered, dream-like, he was keenly aware than his breathing was shallow and fast, as if they were already embracing and kissing and smothering and . . .

"Don't mind the cat."

"Oh. Oh, hi there kitty! You know, I've never really been a cat person." He swallowed painfully; his mouth was dry, his tongue felt swollen, like a giant, dead catfish. "I had a dog once . . . a long time ago . . ."

Stan rattled his head, to get himself back in sync, back in the moment. "But your cat is cute. Is it a boy or girl?"

"Both."

"Um . . . what?"

Before she spoke, she slinked herself onto the sofa, licked her lips. "I've never bothered to look, so both possibilities exist. I didn't want to impose gender roles."

Stan sat down daintily next to her as if the sofa still had the loud, crinkly, plastic covering on it. "Um, wow. That's very deep this early on a Thursday evening."

"Well, I smoke an astronomical amount of weed."

"Ah."

Mary edged closer, slithered closer, temptingly. "I find it's cheaper than cigarettes and less time-consuming than therapy."

"Well, you've clearly thought it all through."

What the hell was he doing here? She was crazy, predatory, unpredictable, she was . . . ohhhhhhh . . .

He had no idea how long he had been there before he finally slid comfortably into small talk, awkwardly making and then breaking eye contact. Eventually, he allowed himself to be led softly by the hand into the dark recess of her bedroom. He just hoped it was true what they said about riding a bicycle. Because he hadn't ridden a bicycle in a really, really long time.

The darkness was absolute; it was like sensory deprivation. Stan banged something painfully against something else savagely. "Ow! It's, uh, awfully dark in here, isn't it?"

"Yeah, well, that makes it romantic."

"Uh . . . okay."

Startled, Stan found himself being thrown violently onto the bed. He was either being mugged or she was aggressively making the first move. Either way, it was a first for him.

"Hey, what are . . . oh . . . hey . . ."

"Ow! My leg—"

"Here, move over . . . no . . . ouch, move . . . no . . . you're pressing on my—ow! . . . *Ow!*"

"Sorry! Hey! No . . . not there . . . that's not what you think it is!"

"But isn't that—?"

"No!"

"Oh, sorry! Ow, ow, ow, ow . . . you're on my hair . . . and not the hair I comb . . ."

"Oh, I'm sorry! Are you okay?"

\* \* \*

Finally, after many years, and several issues of the Victoria's Secret catalog later, he did it. He *did* it. He did it in ways he thought were physically impossible, ways you only heard about happening in underground Amsterdam or back stage at Led Zeppelin concerts. His elbows hurt. His ears were sore. He had learned more about the functions of the male and female anatomy in one very long night than he had ever learned about in school. He might never walk the same again. His yodeling career was definitely over. And yet . . .

And yet, it was a pretty empty feeling. He was cognizant that, through it all, he had been looking for something else, something more meaningful. He had been searching for respect, for acceptance, maybe even for Sarah (not literally, of course, though if he had been, it had been a very *thorough*, albeit unlikely, search). He had been searching for a real connection and found he now felt more alone than ever.

He looked over at Mary's sleeping form, her silhouette making her look like an Egyptian mummy—or, Stan realized much to his surprise, a little bit like Sarah—and gently stroked her shoulder. She eased into wakefulness, and turned.

"Listen . . . I'm sorry if I was a little—"

"Quick?"

"No, I was going to say, I'm sorry if I was a little—"

"Sloppy?"

"No—"

"Clumsy? Small? Unsatisfying?"

"No, I was just going to say I'm sorry if I was a little nervous."

"Oh, were you nervous? I hadn't noticed."

She rubbed the tip of her teeny pug nose ever so softly against his. It felt great; not just her nose against his, the smell of her hitting him full in the face, but the fact that she was the only person since the show's success who had the nerve to tease him, to treat him like he was an ordinary person.

They lay silently together just looking at each other. Stan was pleasantly surprised just how comfortable and relaxed he felt, even with her elbow, innocently, wedging its way painfully into his liver. With her innocent clumsiness, being with her was more like being with Sarah than he was comfortable with. In fact, he had only just now realized, even her perfume, her scent, was the same as Sarah's . . .

Stan was enjoying the serenity, the silence, but could sense her itching curiosity—the insatiable curiosity of a cat—there was clearly something she wanted to ask him. Admiring her, confidently lying there, unashamed of her nakedness, not even the corner of a tattered bedsheet covering her, he gave her a small nod and raised his eyebrows: go ahead, ask.

"So . . . about the show . . . what do you think about—"

Stan sat up so quickly he was mildly dizzy. "Whoa. Stop right there. Let's not talk about the show. Please."

She placed her hand on his heart, eased him back down on the bed. "Okay . . . okay . . ."

Mary looked up at the ceiling with a thoughtful expression as if she could see straight through it and deep into the night sky itself. "But . . . I don't understand why you don't want to talk about . . . Stan, the show means everything to me. I've found that the love of millions of distant strangers is far better than the love of any one person up close. And I couldn't possibly give it up now. I would do anything for the good of the show."

"It's hard to explain . . . I guess it's a . . . sinking feeling. Knowing that people spend years creating a beautiful picture or a book of poetry. And maybe, *maybe*, a few dozen people ever experience it. I prance around and act like an animal and millions watch me every week."

This was far better than sex. He could think of dozens—maybe even hundreds, if he was honest—of women he wanted to sleep with. But he could only imagine a very small number of women he would want to just lay and talk to. Of course, the weed was helping enormously; he was higher than Icelandic inflation.

At first, she had suggested it just to loosen him up a bit and he was too embarrassed to admit he had never smoked before, he had never done anything before, really. He didn't even drink coffee, he wanted each experience to be his own, he couldn't condone an artificial feeling, an artificial emotion. But having acquiesced, he found the drug had loosened his back, his shoulders, his neck, and then it had loosened his lips. It had eased his mind as well as his conscience, for once making him not so anxious, so neurotic, so overly critical of everything. He was enjoying the free association, the ease of the conversation.

Mary idly scratched her arm, as if her itching curiosity had physically manifested itself. She gently prodded again, "But . . . you're living every actor's dream? Why do you hate it so much? I see you, during rehearsals, during recordings, standing there like . . . like you're standing on your own grave. Like you've committed the worst possible crime and are praying to get caught so you don't have to live with the guilt."

Gradually, they had become intertwined, and Stan absently rubbed at an exposed expanse of flesh, barely aware of where she stopped and he began, "It's more than just guilt. There's the pressure. The responsibility. Feeling like so many people are depending on me to perform. You, Nigel . . . my . . . my old . . . I know someone who is in need of some money, for an operation. I'm not always so good with responsibility."

Mary shifted away just a few inches but Stan could feel a little growing distance. "So . . . I guess you've never considered marriage or kids, then?"

Stan shifted, considered confessing how, at times, just looking at a child made him want to weep: for their potential, their innocence, their endless options; he could weep for all that he himself had missed, all that he himself had lost. Instead, he muttered, "I can't even imagine that. Even when I was an actor, I couldn't play a husband or father convincingly. Besides, I wouldn't want to bring up children in a world where someone like me is considered a success. Plus, do you have any idea just how expensive kids are? How much work they are? When they're small, you have to feed them almost *every* day. And I don't have a great track record with responsibility. Houseplants, goldfish, pet rocks, imaginary friends . . . anything or anyone depending on me never stood a chance."

"But you used to have a dog, didn't you? You took care of him—"

"He didn't rely on me, I relied on him. I don't want to talk about it."

Stan turned away, nearly sank his teeth into the pillow, remembering his dog. "I guess . . . I guess it isn't responsibility that scares me so much as . . ."

Stan drifted off, magnetized by the lure of the moonlight through the window, and several minutes passed quietly, as if he didn't even realize he hadn't finished the thought; eventually, he mumbled, "The easiest thing in the world is to care about someone. The harder thing, the infinitely harder thing, to do is to not care. But when you do care about someone . . . you worry about them. Worry about them leaving you. Worry about them not loving you anymore. Worry about them crossing the street. The anxiety is unbearable."

She nestled into him and they had several minutes, perhaps hours, of pleasant silence. Stan made a conscious effort to mark this occasion, to do something people often said or thought about but never actually did: enjoy this moment, savor the time you spend with those you care about, because you never know; it could all be over quicker than you think.

"Would you like to do something again tomorrow?"

Sleepily, Stan confessed, yawning, "You know, I've never watched the sunrise. Always meant to, but I've never made the time."

"Then we'll do that. Tomorrow morning. And every morning after that."

# Chapter 14

They didn't get up early the next morning to watch the sunrise or, as it turned out, any morning after that. But it had only taken that one night of excruciating marathon sex and Mary was a nearly permanent fixture in Stan's life: a spare toothbrush on his bathroom sink, a few random drawers emptied out for her, giving her a set of keys. Stan found her enthusiasm irresistible; like a neighborhood stray cat, she had no respect for emotional or real estate boundaries. They were practically inseparable. When she left his house, her perfume clung on the air for hours afterward, and he would literally hug the air, as if embracing the essence that she left behind. And he found himself, more frequently and louder than he would normally have dared, smiling to himself as he hummed popular boy band songs.

The press, in their ever-increasing desire to simplify things to the point of stupidity, had even blessed the happy couple with a mono plume, an unholy Orwellian mashing of two words—or in the case of celebrity couples, two names—into one: SchröLov.

And tonight, like swarms of gnats, the paparazzi were out in full force, as Mary hung on Stan's arm like an expensive wristwatch. A crowd of fans, packed in like battery hens, stretched and reached for him feverishly, like blitzed bleacher bums grasping madly for a foul ball, as if one touch would have some magical healing power. As they approached the church, the last thing Stan expected was for a photographer to step up and punch him the face.

Stan pinched his nose, half-heartedly searched the pavement for his shattered eyeglasses, while several dozen predatory photographers reeled off snap after snap in a blinding strobe of flashes. Stan asked accusingly, "Hey! What in de hell was dat fo'?"

"That? That was for being an inconsiderate douchebag and

not having better names to combine!"

Tentatively, he released the bridge of his nose, leaned his head back slightly, in case he was still bleeding. "What in de holy hell are yo' talkin' 'bout?"

Jostling, elbow to elbow, against his fellow photographers, he framed up Stan in his camera crosshairs. "'SchröLov'? Ridiculous! Next time find a woman's whose name better integrates into your own—asshole!"

Stan had often fantasized about exacting physical violence against the photographers but he was shocked to be reverse Sean Penned.

If Stan was surprised by the assault, it wasn't half as surprising as being invited to Comb Over's wedding.

For one thing, he would have bet his left and right kidneys that Comb Over and Blow Dry were gayer than Freddie Mercury marching in the St. Patrick's Day Parade. For another, he hadn't expected to be considered a friend. Looking around, he noticed practically everyone from the show was already here; rather than seating one side or the other by bride or groom, they had naturally aligned themselves by grips and electrics or by art, hair, make-up; when he made eye contact, they nodded, reverentially, in his direction, beaming as if his nose wasn't swollen, as if he didn't have a lingering smear of blood tracing a thin, jagged pink line down his face.

The idea of marriage had never appealed; for a man whose every waking moment had been, for such a long time, dedicated to being someone else—taking on different accents, personalities, classes, desires, motivations—it seemed unreasonable. How could he know who he was and what he wanted—let alone provide a stable personality to someone else—when he had no idea whom he was going to be from day to day? But, in the peaceful stillness of the church, with Mary by his side, he wondered . . .

"Stan!" someone yelled out, the loud echo bounding around

the church hall like the sound of buckshot.

Balled fists held up in front of his face, like a washed-up boxer, fearing another assault, Stan yelled, "Jesus!"

Comb Over was leering behind him; in his perfectly creased tuxedo he looked like an eight-track cassette tape: chunky, clunky, impractical.

Stan stood up, but only halfway, for once in his life trying to not draw too much attention to himself. "What are you doing here? You're supposed to be getting married right now."

Straightening an already ruler-straight bow tie, Comb Over laughed, "Stanny Boy . . . I'm fully aware of my impending marriage. That can wait a few minutes. As you know, our initial agreement was only for twelve weeks. But now that the show's a success and it has been picked up for a full season, we need to talk to you about renewing your contract."

And then, popping up into Stan's eye line like a muppet, Blow Dry appeared, holding out an unscrupulous pen and the contract in question. Stan was keenly aware that everyone was staring at them. "What? No . . . not now, get the hell out of here. Get on up there and get married. We'll talk later, for Christ's sake."

"Stan . . ."

"No!" And then as softly as he possibly could, so as not to offend anyone who might actually be here for the wedding, he whispered, "Fuck off."

"All right. Listen, just sit back, relax, enjoy the show. We'll chat again before the cake-cutting scene, okay?"

Even though Comb Over was speaking at full volume, Stan was still trying to maintain some degree of decorum and whispered, "Ceremony. In real life it's called a *ceremony*, not a scene."

Comb Over shrugged. "Hey, whatever. You say 'to-*may*-to', I say 'to-*may*-to'."

Gritting his teeth, Stan whispered, "You are a complete idiot."

"Sorry, what?"

"I said, 'You scare the fucking hell out of me!'"

Comb Over, somehow taking this as a sign of encouragement, gave Stan two crooked thumbs-up and headed confidently to the altar.

\* \* \*

Stan missed most of the actual ceremony; he was signing autographs for the ushers and the less engaged members of the wedding party. What he did catch was something that at one time would have sounded like a load of empty promises, bits of poetry, a few outright lies, and a whole wheelbarrow full of religious nonsense. And Stan suspected, for someone like Comb Over, it probably was—just an expensive public celebration of a personal financial merger, a union of wealth disguised under the auspices of love.

Stan was distracted from this line of thought when he recognized the show announcer sitting, alone, at a reception table. They had never spoken before, partly because Stan couldn't stomach the fact that someone had an even easier, lazier job than he did and partly because he had a deep, gnawing, nagging suspicion that, one dreadful afternoon, the announcer had done the unthinkable and stolen his lunch from the communal fridge. The investigation proved inconclusive but the suspicion was enough. Since that day onward, his lunch was now religiously handcuffed to the scrawny wrist of a hopeful, sometimes reluctant, intern until Stan was hungry.

But Stan knew something was wrong. The announcer didn't have his typical optimistic swagger. He didn't have his back-pocket smile. He didn't have his fly zipped, either, but, given the state he was clearly in, Stan decided not to mention it. He approached him and put his hand on his shoulder. "Hey, are you okay? You look . . . well . . . you look terrible."

"They . . . fired me." He pointed a shaking, accusing finger in

Comb Over and Blow Dry's general direction.

"What happened?"

"I told them I wanted to do something a little more challenging. That I was ready to take the next step up, do something a little more fulfilling. That what I was doing was so menial that a monkey could do my job."

"So . . . what did they say?"

"They said, 'My God, you're right.' Fired me on the spot."

Stan flashed his hands to his mouth, as if he were afraid he was going to be violently sick. It could just as easily have been him; not that he would have cared, not that he didn't dream of being set free: it was simply the idea, the startling validation, of how ruthless this business was. Faintly, through his clasped fingers, he whispered, "Jesus."

"By the time I got back to my desk to pack up my stuff, someone was delivering a pallet of bananas. They said I could still come to the wedding, though, so I could make a few new connections."

Blow Dry jumped up and down in Stan's eye line. Stan cupped his hands over his eyes, pretending he couldn't see him.

"Stan! Hey, Stan!"

Blow Dry continued to try and flag him down . . . was he really still believing, unbelievably, that Stan didn't see or hear him?

"Stanny Boy!"

"Hey . . . listen . . . we'll talk about this some more, okay? I'll come find you later."

That was a lie. Not an intentional lie, but a lie nonetheless. Stan forgot about the announcer, would never think about him again, from almost the moment he stood up, trying to find a means of escape. The flickering, brash light of the men's room beckoned and he ran . . .

He was relieved, as he began to relieve himself, with the pleasant whiteness and the silence of his new sanctuary before:

"Pretty small, huh?"

"Excuse me?" Stan was disgusted to see Nigel had come right up against him and stood at the urinal next to him, violating the unwritten rule of men.

Stan didn't know what Nigel could possibly be doing to himself over there, he was flailing both hands frantically, like he was performing semaphore, inebriated; it was unnerving. "The camera crew. The press. I would have thought with you here, there would be a lot more media activity. Hey, is now a bad time to talk about your contract extension?"

Stan whirled a full ninety degrees, making Nigel jump.

"Hey!"

"Oh, sorry."

As Nigel, pants now dripping wet, ran to the sink and tried to aim his lap under the automatic hand dryer, which made far more noise than heat, Comb Over and Blow Dry materialized on either side of Stan.

"Seriously, though," Blow Dry began, "I have a pen right here . . ."

"Not *now!*"

"Listen, Stan," Comb Over jumped in, "there was just one other thing we wanted to discuss with you."

"Jesus! Can't a guy just take a freakin' — "

"It's about Tom." Blow Dry said.

"Who the hell is Tom?" Stan asked, while shaking it so hard it hurt.

"Who's Tom?" Comb Over laughed. "Stan, you're funny." And everyone laughed — and stopped laughing — in perfect sync.

"Tom, of course," Blow Dry said, "is the very popular reigning champion of *Animal Instinct.*"

They had followed Stan to the sink, where he ripped and strangled the paper towels like he wished he could do to—

"And we'd like it stay that way . . . at least through sweeps week . . . you know what we mean?" Comb Over asked, weighing his hand heavily on Stan's back, leaving a small, cold, wet puddle.

"You're . . . asking me to cheat?"

"'Cheat' is a strong accusation," Blow Dry warned. "Think about whether that's really what you're suggesting."

Stan stared up into the fluorescent lights, listened hard to their harmonic hum. "Yeah, yeah . . . I've thought about it, that's exactly what I'm suggesting that you're suggesting. And the answer is 'no.'"

"Stan—"

Nigel tried to get Stan's attention. "There is just one other thing I wanted to ask you about, if you have a sec—"

After an intricate balancing act that ensured he didn't in fact touch anything with bare skin, Stan raced out of the men's room, feeling queasy. He saw that Mary was making her rounds, greeting everyone as if it were her wedding, but she made sure to catch his eye every now and again. And he never failed to notice; he could barely take his eyes off of her.

Nigel, bellying his way up to Stan, and still trying unsuccessfully to get his pants dry with a linen napkin he had stolen right off the lap of a passing guest, said, "I know you can't convincingly fake that lovelorn look—or we would have landed at least one of those soap opera auditions. I'm not sure I like the way you're looking at Mary. Just remember: getting married is the single stupidest thing a guy could do."

Stan gave Nigel a knowing look.

"Okay, okay . . . studying liberal arts is the stupidest thing a guy could do, but marriage is close. Listen, I'm all in favor of you two being together . . . it's good for the show. And the show is everything. But we want to keep it no strings attached."

Nigel, probably subconsciously, put his hands in his pockets, as if he were checking that his wallet was as full and thickly packed as he remembered. "The two of you getting . . . *too* serious . . . would make things . . . well . . . it would add a whole new complexity to the accounting, you see what I mean? Let's not rush into anything, huh?"

Stan looked at his waxy shoes, idly squeaked them on the floor. "But . . . she likes me."

"So?"

"So, that's a quality I find really attractive in a woman."

"Jesus Christ—"

Stan closed his eyes tight, as if he could see the words written large on a cue card in his mind. "Honestly Nigel, to tell the truth for one brief moment, she means the world to me. And I can't stand being alone anymore. Ever since Sarah left I've making it with a box of Kleenex."

"Seems reasonable. Practical, even. Get off and clean up at the same time."

"It's just . . . she's the person I want to talk to every night before I go to sleep."

Stan had never seen Nigel blush before, but there he was, his stubbly cheeks slowly pulsing red, like he was reacting to poison sumac. It was repulsive, it was enough to even put a fat man off his slice of wedding cake . . . if it wasn't for the fact that Comb Over's wedding cake was *Swiss chocolate buttercream*, there was no way Stan was going to pass that up. But he would only have one slice . . . maybe he would have a little of Mary's if she didn't finish hers . . . or maybe when she wasn't looking . . .

"Let's put this aside for just a moment." Nigel was all business again. Or, more realistically, as he always was. "About this new contract—"

Mary had meandered her way over. "Stan, could I . . . borrow . . . you for a moment?"

Interlocking her slender fingers through his, she led him . . . he didn't know where, but it didn't matter, as long as he was with her, it didn't matter; the fact that, wherever they were going, was away from Nigel was just an added bonus. One week. Just one more week, he would have more than enough money for the dog's operation, his contract would expire, and he would be free . . . free to spend his days with her . . . his nights . . .

She dabbed at the remaining dried blood under his nose; it hurt far more than it helped, but he had no intention of dissuading her touch.

They had to shout to be heard over the music now, and Mary, effortlessly, was swaying and shouted in his ear: "Let's dance!"

Stan stood rooted to the floor as if his shoes were made of lead. Just the thought of getting out on the dance floor made him feel like he had a mouthful of sand. He envied people who could do it. He could never get the hang of it. Give him someone else's words to say, a costume to hide behind, a character to hide within, and he would revel in the spotlight. But to have to be himself, to have nothing but his own body to rely on, to be in his own skin, having to improvise and express who he was in a public setting—that was beyond him. For Stan, dancing wasn't an involuntary gesture, something his body just did in reaction to the music. It was a conscious effort, a monumental force of will, so much so that he could only focus on moving one body part at a time.

First, he would wildly jerk his neck back, as if he had a giant mosquito between his shoulder blades that he was trying to squash with the back of his head. Then he would stand on one leg and shake the other as if he were trying to dislodge a swarm of bees out of his pants. This would inevitably be followed by voraciously thrusting his pelvis like he was Mick Jagger on Viagra. Spectators would evacuate the dance floor, ideally in a calm and orderly fashion, ensuring women and children got to safety first.

So he simply stood on the sidelines and watched her, admired her, entranced by every effortless move her body made, hypnotizing him with her movement and rhythm. She was closing her eyes now, and waving her arms as if she were gently treading water, and everyone else simply faded away as she telescoped closer and closer in his vision. A revelation hit him. How foolish he was to be so worried about everything all the time. How lucky he was to have what he had; how lucky he was just to know her; how lucky he was just to be alive!

Stan saw her as just a colorful blur, leaving a time trail behind her, as if she transcended time itself. He ran out to join her, not caring how he looked, and threw himself into it in a fit of uncoordinated and clumsy joy. He found, for the first time in quite a while, no one was looking at him; it was just him and her, sharing this one moment in time, communicating only with their movements. Windmilling his arms like Pete Townshend after a dozen vodka tonics, Stan was a sweaty mess, hair plastered to his face, shirt untucked, heart beating hard in double time to the beat. It was glorious. It would be like this every night. Well, they wouldn't be at a hundred-thousand-dollar wedding with several hundred guests and a band every night that would be a bit silly. No. But every night would be this exhilarating, doing things that maybe made him a little uncomfortable, appreciating every sound and movement she made, feeling like they were the only two people on the face of the Earth.

He could do anything with her by his side. He would be invincible. He could fly. He could defy gravity. He could travel in time. He could even get jiggy with it, he would just need to be careful not to throw out his back.

He whispered gently in her ear, "I realize now, it's become clear just this minute, you are the only thing I ever wanted. You've made me happier than I ever imagined possible. It would take me the rest of my life to repay you and if you'd let me, I'd very much like the opportunity to try."

"Sorry, what?"

"I said, 'marry me'!"

Mary pulled suggestively on his tie, bringing him achingly close. He could feel her cool breath right on his face; it lightly brushed the hair from his forehead.

"Sign the contract and we'll talk!" And she gave him a long, hard kiss, leered at him. For a brief flickering moment, he thought, maybe, he caught a hint of fangs in her sinister smile. Stan's blood froze and the world fell away.

# Chapter 15

He knew now there was, truly, no one left in the wicked world he could trust.

His coolness, their rumored break-up, was that week's big news. He was tired of all the questions and the calls about Mary, the calls from Mary; he had simply stopped picking up the phone and eventually, she went quietly into that good night, the two staying cordial and professional on the studio floor, but the chemistry they had had together was simply gone, something that was readily apparent to even the most ardent, and brain-dead, fan.

He couldn't have defined exactly where it was, but there was a physical pain, an open wound, that Sarah's absence had created and, he thought, only Mary might have been able to heal; but didn't.

\* \* \*

Stan was shocked when he realized that, buried deep in the tiny fine print of his contract—which, other than the dollar amount, he didn't bother to read—were the binding, deadly words committing him to a dizzying schedule of publicity servitude. It was Nigel's proficiency, his masterstroke, devising a whirlwind tour to rival that of the heaviest heavy metal band. And Stan meekly obeyed, rolled over on Nigel's command, because . . . what else did he have to do, whom did he have to go home to?

Thankful for any distraction, making the best of it all, he was pleased to find himself in a crowded bookstore. Stan loved the way that you could lose all sense and perspective of time when in a bookstore, like you could in a smoky casino or in a Midwestern shopping mall or like waiting in line at the DMV. He wanted to get lost in the aisles, wending his way through the endless trails, but he knew no matter how far he explored, there was just no possible escape from Nigel's machinations.

Nigel could have sold the recipe for ice to Eskimos on a royalty percentage in perpetuity, living comfortably off the compounding interest. But even for Nigel, this was impressive. Stan had been shocked and shaken the first time he saw a recording of himself on TV. All the years of hoping and fantasizing hadn't even begun to prepare him for it. But now, seeing his giant face stretched across a taut poster announcing that Stan was giving a book signing "today only," was a real surprise. Especially since he hadn't written anything.

To Nigel, that was no more than a minor nuisance. When it came to an opportunity for promotion, for publicity, for money, Nigel was unstoppable.

Timidly, Stan sat down, as if the chair might fall to dust beneath his weight. The applause, the sound of applause that rained down as he entered, no longer meant anything to him, had become no more than simply white noise. He couldn't concentrate on what anyone said or did, and he was suddenly surprised to find himself face-to-face with an eager fan, a hardcover book thrown in front of him and everyone waiting, waiting for him to do something.

"Uh . . . this is *David Copperfield*? I didn't write this."

Nigel leaned over, just like the devil on his shoulder that he was. "You've read it, haven't you?"

"Well, yeah, I have, but—"

"That's good enough for me. Sign it, smile, and keep this line moving."

This was crazy. Not a single person was questioning this. As the morning wore on, Stan had signed, among others, works by literary giants like Nabokov, Dostoevsky, London, and Woolf. As the absurdity of the situation became more and more normal, Stan started writing personalized messages that bordered on the pornographic. He could do anything, anything at all now . . .

He was starting to enjoy himself when he was jarred painfully back to reality; one of his favorite books was plunked on the table in front of him: a battered, weathered copy of Kurt Vonnegut's *Mother Night*. It was as if someone had thrown a bucket of ice water in his face; it embarrassed him, it highlighted the contrast of what he was against a great work of literature. He didn't deserve to be in the same room as this book.

He looked up to see who had done this to him, who had played this cruel trick, and he saw one of the most beautiful sights he had ever seen, her face lit up by a toothy and slightly lopsided smile.

Stan grinned despite himself, opened the book and signed his name without ever breaking eye contact. He handed her the book and confessed, "This is his best, I think. Such a brave story. Hopefully, taught me a thing or two."

She closed her eyes, pressed the book against her chest with both hands, as if giving it a small, tight hug, and quoted the moral of the story as outlined by Vonnegut himself: "'We are what we pretend to be so we must be careful about who we pretend to be.'"

"Sorry, what was your name again?"

"I'm Hope."

"You sure are."

Hope laughed, self-consciously covered her mouth. He didn't want to, he really didn't want to, but he couldn't help but stare. Stan motioned for her to give him back the book. "I forgot to inscribe it for you." He spoke out loud as he wrote, "To Hope: remember the moral of the story."

As he gave her back the book once again, their hands brushed tenderly against each other, and he wondered feverishly if it had been accidental or deliberate. He prayed she would say something, anything . . .

Nigel motioned violently for the employees managing the line to bring the next person through; the grinding machine of business had an annoying grain of sand stopping up the works. In a fleeting moment, she was gone.

The hours, and then the day, just evaporated as did, eventually, the picture-perfect image of her face. By the time the signing was over, all that remained was the fuzzy recollection of her general features and the disturbing, nagging, cold fear that maybe, just maybe, she hadn't even been real . . .

# Chapter 16

To Stan, newspapers were the ultimate prop. They could convey a wide array of intent and emotion. Tonight, he was using one to convey amateur stealth and poorly concealed anxiety. He held the paper suspiciously high to cover his nervous face and he gripped it so tight that his fingernails made little rip ripples through to the sections below. In a romantic ideal of mystery and cloak-and-dagger, in the late-night, darkened corner of a barely used parking lot, he had arranged for the newspaper to be the tip-off to the young lady he was scheduled to meet tonight.

But there was also the practical aspect to keeping a low profile, burrowing under shadows, now that he was so recognizable. He didn't mind the autographs; in fact, even after all this time, he was still flattered. He no longer minded the persistent attention or the fact that he couldn't even have five minutes to himself. What had become so difficult was living up to what people expected of him, that everyone wanted him to be so much more interesting and witty that he could ever be, that, somehow, money and fame had made him smarter, wiser, deeper . . . Stan felt about as deep as a peeling bumper sticker on the back of a rusty red pickup truck.

"Hello, Stan."

If he was startled out of his reverie, he was a consummate enough performer not to let it show. He made a point of reading a full sentence before he looked up from his newspaper. "Hello, Sarah."

The sight of her, the thick hit of her perfume, made time stand still and then, inexplicably, unravel backward; each sweet memory, frozen in a mental Polaroid, made him ache. He shook his head, to shake off the memories, to wake up back in the present. Leaning against his car, he tried, unsuccessfully, to look and sound nonchalant. "You haven't aged a single day. You look just as beautiful as the day you left. That is just downright rude of you."

There was no crack in her poker-faced facade; Sarah simply held out her hand for the check.

Crossing his arms he hugged himself, wishing it was her. "Have you . . . uh . . . have you seen my show?"

"What show?"

"What do you mean, 'what show'? It's the biggest thing on television—"

Sarah smiled. "I'm kidding. I've been meaning to watch it but haven't had the chance yet. I've been watching that show where people fall down and hurt themselves."

"Which one?"

"I'm gonna record your show, though. Looking forward to seeing it."

"Well, you had better do it soon. I won't be doing the show for much longer. I no longer have any reason to."

Stan could tell Sarah longed to say something but that she couldn't think of anything to say. He decided to bail her out; true to who he had always been, he preferred when he had most of the lines. "So, where's my dog?"

"He isn't well enough to travel. He's at home. With a nurse. I was able to get him a full-time nurse."

"Ah."

Turning to hide tears he feared but never came . . . he . . . he . . . damn it, would they never be reunited? Would he never feel complete again?

"But he is doing okay, though? The treatments are helping?"

"He's doing much better. Eating better. Playing with his toys. He even started shitting on freshly mowed lawns again."

"Aw. That always made us all laugh."

"Yeah."

"Yeah."

Stan knew this was unfair to Sarah, that he could have just

handed over the check and been done with it. Or he could have mailed it—spending forty cents on a stamp rather than four hundred dollars to fly her out to LA, but he had insisted on doing this in person, keenly aware that the drama of the late-night parking lot hand-off still somehow appealed to his former self.

"So . . . no more proper acting, huh?"

Stan took a step closer to her, straining to re-memorize her features in the dim light, cognizant this could be the last time he ever saw her; he missed having her to confide in. "After you both left I tried to keep a toehold in the business. I was the backup weatherman for Channel Eleven Action News. It was good experience: acting in front of a blue screen, special effects experience, stage all to myself. Decent lines. But after a while I found myself quietly plotting accidents for the main weatherman so I could get more airtime. Never went through with anything, of course, but it made me start to think that maybe, just maybe, acting wasn't so healthy for me. I didn't want anything to do with acting anymore, not even something as benign as being a game show host. But . . . for the dog . . . well, so here we are. You seeing anyone?"

The abrupt change of subject made Sarah jump. When she said nothing, Stan changed tack. "Well, I just want you to know, I met someone recently and something happened. Well, something happened for me, I don't know if something happened for her."

"Ohhhhh. You had sex."

His laugh was so loud and unexpected he couldn't control himself from snorting and, embarrassed, quickly covered his face with both hands. He said, muffled, "Okay, okay . . . touché."

The check suddenly was a millstone in his pocket. He just wanted to get rid of it; he held it out to Sarah, ashamed of his ill-begotten wealth. "Well . . . here's the check. Tell him . . . tell him I said *woof*. He'll know."

She took the check and folded it neatly, placing it in her purse like it was a delicate and priceless piece of origami. She turned to go, got halfway to her car; Stan felt his heart diminish to ash. "Wait! Wait . . . maybe I could help with the cost of the nurse, too, maybe send the occasional check to help make him more comfortable, to make sure he's happy?"

Sarah stopped, keeping her back turned to him. "Sure, that would be great, but I thought you said you weren't going to—"

"And maybe I could see him once in a while? Like . . . visitation rights?"

She turned to him; for one brief moment, he thought maybe, she might reconcile, ask him to come back and they could all go back to the way things were . . . before. . . . "Maybe. Once in a while. I guess that would be okay."

There it was . . . a glimmer, just a glimmer of hope, a chance to see his dog again . . . he would do whatever it took . . . Sarah was saying something else; he could see her lips moving, had to concentrate hard to hear her say, "Can I give you some advice?"

He cupped his hands to his mouth even though she was only a few feet away, said louder than he intended, "Will it cost me anything?"

"You have to stop looking for the lightning bolt to strike, stop waiting for some mythical perfect person, perfect job. Just find someone you like being with, someone you have something in common with, and just let yourself be happy."

She turned her collar to the wind and got in her car while Stan stood, his mouth half-open, Sarah's parting words sinking in like spilled milk into a shag carpet. He was running full tilt toward Hope's house before Sarah had closed her car door.

# Chapter 17

It took Stan three seconds to realize he didn't know where Hope lived but another three hours before he gave up looking. He was winded, he was lost, he was wet from the lightly falling rain, but it didn't matter.

His initial enthusiasm had turned to burning obsession, which, as with most obsessions, eventually burned itself out, and he found himself simply going through the motions of looking for her when he wasn't rehearsing or recording or doing publicity. Days had turned to weeks had turned to months; an entire season came and went. He found himself suspiciously frequenting the bookstore where they had met, like a criminal returning to the scene of the crime to try and recapture the thrill.

Stately, plump, Stan Pavlov left that same damn bookstore, yet again, in a haze, and was mildly shocked to find himself suddenly at the trendy bar next door, awakened from his bland and unmemorable daydream by a passing patron who asked for his autograph on a dirty cocktail napkin. Among the wet splooge of beer, shaped like an exotic island, Stan left his celebrity signature on that napkin, an impressionistic squiggle within which the best handwriting experts the world had to offer would have had trouble identifying a single letter.

He had thirty minutes until he was due on set. No matter how he felt about this job, a deal was a deal and he was still, if nothing else, a professional. A man was only as good as his word, as good as the promises he kept. If, in all those years, his father had only bothered to teach Stan one simple lesson, he might as well comply.

He would have just one drink. And he would leave in ten minutes, giving him ample time to get to the studio.

The bartender approached Stan and with a nudge he chided, "Hey, kid. Cheer up. You're young. You've got your whole life ahead of you."

Stan considered that for a moment and then whacked his head on the bar, repeatedly.

"Hey! Hey! Be careful, that's worth quite a bit of money."

Stan stopped and the room swam in and out and then back in to focus again in a matter of moments. "Doesn't matter. I could do my job even with half the amount of brain cells. With a quarter of them, I could be a contestant."

"I'm not talking about your damn fool head, I'm talkin' 'bout my bar. That's real sandalwood, all one piece."

"It's . . . it's nice."

The bartender caressed the top of his bar lovingly, like stroking a beloved pet. "Go on, feel it."

Stan slid off his stool, stumbled and slurred a bit. "Thanks but . . . it's time I was going . . ."

"Wait, hang on. I see you going into that bookstore almost every day. Did you lose something in there or something?"

"Yeah. Yeah, I think I probably did."

As Stan slumped his head, looked down as far as he could look down, he realized that no matter how wealthy and well-known he became, no matter how much money he spent, his shoes would always look shabby, shameful, pitiful; it was as if something in the way he walked, guilty and weighted, caused him to drag his feet, as if they were questioning wherever he wanted to go.

"Never understood the appeal of books, myself. We used to have a bartender here, named Hope, always carried around a stack of books and—"

Even the shattering sound of his glass exploding as it dropped and hit the sticky, tacky floor couldn't break his focus. "What . . . what did you say her name was?"

\* \* \*

He wasted several precious minutes deciding if he should go. If he was fast, really lightning-round fast, he could go to her, give her his pitch, make a date, and still be back in time to record the show.

Panting for breath, he had no idea what he was going to say. Who knew if she'd even remember that small, meager moment they had shared, months ago? Who knew if it had even been as memorable to her, as it had been to Stan?

He finally got to the address the barman had given him; it was a vaguely rundown apartment complex, and, winded far more than he cared to admit to himself, he leaned against the mailbox out front while he tried to catch his elusive breath. He looked nervously at his watch. Okay, no time to catch his breath, he'd have to worry about that later.

He chucked himself against the lobby door, uncaring of the consequences, pleased as well as slightly embarrassed, when it turned out the door was unlocked and opened inward; he took several faltering steps before awkwardly regaining his balance.

Okay. No elevator. *Fuckity, fuckity, fuckity,* he thought in perfect rhythm with his pounding heart as he bounced up all seven flights of stairs, and hurled himself at her front door, repeatedly. He looked intensely at his watch again: at best, he had about three minutes to do this.

"Hey . . . hey! Open up! Listen . . . sorry . . . I don't have a lot of time but . . . I . . . just haven't been able to stop thinking about you."

Talking was taking more out of him than he had anticipated and he leaned heavily against the doorframe and clutched at his chest. "Please. I just . . . I just want . . . to see your face again. Just for a moment . . ."

A befuddled fifty-something man, his reading glasses perched clumsily on the end of his nose, opened the door, just a fraction. "Um . . . can I help you?"

Hope, who had been standing, arms crossed, in her doorframe

across the hall for most of the performance, coughed politely. "Stan? I live over here."

"Oh."

As Stan turned to go, the man gently pinched Stan's shirt-sleeve with his thumb and forefinger. "Does that mean you take back what you said?"

"Well, I—"

"Staaaan!" Hope warned.

"Right, right . . . coming . . ."

He let himself be led into her apartment, but he didn't notice anything other than her light blue eyes, which were so pale it looked like someone had forgotten to finish coloring them in. His eyes were drawn relentlessly to her bottom lip—pink and proud—jutting out slightly like a window ledge. She had ruler-straight hair—it was quite a bit shorter than he'd remembered—that couldn't decide if it was blond or brunette and wasn't going to be making a commitment any time soon. And major, major jugs. Seriously, you could lose a bicycle pump in there.

He tried to straighten himself, his untucked clothes, his wild hair.

"So, what were you saying—"

Stan was too tired to even hold up a hand; he gradually bent over, silently cursing the nagging stitch in his side. "No, don't speak . . . sorry, listen . . . I have about . . . two minutes, tops . . . so I don't have time to do this suave or coy . . . which . . . I'm not anyway. I'm just . . . glad to have found you."

She laughed at this and opened her mouth to speak, but Stan was on a tight schedule. "Sorry . . . only about a minute . . . and a half left . . . so, have to . . . do this quick. What do you do?"

"I'm an aspiring actress."

It was as if Stan had been shot in the back. He threw his head back and let out a very loud groan, nearly wept.

Hope roped her delicate hands around his arm. "I was just kidding."

"Oh, thank Christ—"

"I'm a student. I was bartending for a bit, but now I'm back to school full-time. I'm studying—"

"Ah!" Stan put a finger over her lips. "Don't tell me too much or we'll have nothing to talk about on a date . . . and I only have about forty-five seconds left. So . . . what do you think?"

If she was thrown by this unconventional courtship, she had the poise not to show it. She shrugged, but flirtatiously. "Sure . . . Friday?"

"Well, I may need to fly to San Diego on Friday to continue my publicity tour . . ."

Hands squirming in his pockets, fumbling, as if he were holding a weapon or searching desperately for his lines, Stan spoke softly. "Or . . . I may skip it and stick around, I haven't decided. But . . . if I do stick around, you would really meet me for a drink?"

"Yeah. Of course I would."

"Then I have definitely decided. Listen, let me give you my number, that way it's totally in your hands."

Stan scribbled his number quickly, his hands shaky, placing the scrap of paper in her palm with both of his hands, closing her fingers around it securely.

"Well, great then. Great. Is there a bad time to call you? I mean, times when you've recording the show or . . ."

"There could never be a bad time for you to call me."

He kissed her, timidly, on the cheek and ran down the stairs two at a time. True to his word, Stan sprinted to set and made it on time, with less than a minute to spare. If there was one thing the former aspiring actor could appreciate, it was good timing.

# Chapter 18

Stan's head started throbbing the moment that he signed his new contract and hadn't stopped since. His contract had more commas in it than a sentence in a James Joyce novel and it made his eyes swim to try and read it. He still couldn't believe he had signed it, after all the time he spent counting down the days until he would be free.

Stan stood, rubbing his forehead, with Nigel, watching the whitewashed drizzle and driving rain, as they huddled together under the awning of the studio's main entrance. It had been a tough day, a long day's recording; another episode where he cheated to ensure that the reigning champion, Tom, won. If a man's convictions fall in a studio and no one else cares, do they make a noise?

"Stan, listen, there's a small favor I've been meaning to talk to you about—"

Nigel was interrupted by Mary, shivering against the cold and wet, as she literally bumped into them. She wedged herself between them in the dim, last dying rays of light. Her accidental touch, brushed against his arm, repulsed Stan, like an unidentified insect crawling on sunburned skin.

Mary clearly didn't sense how drastically his feelings had changed and her naivety made Stan even more annoyed, even angrier. If he'd had any respect for her, it now had evaporated completely; he could never respect someone who didn't pick up their cues.

She touched his arm again, deliberately this time, and Stan jumped back as if her fingertips shot electricity out of their overly preened fingernails. "Do you have an umbrella I can borrow?"

"No."

"But . . . what's that in your hand?"

"It's not an umbrella."

But it was. "But. . ."

He glared at her, through her, as if daring her to contradict him.

She shuddered slightly. "Hey, I'm sorry . . . I'm sorry for how everything went down. I really am. But listen, if you want to get together, maybe talk about how to incorporate that new routine into the show . . . or, if you . . . you know . . ."

Balling his fists, knuckle white, he took a threatening step in her direction. "No. No, I don't know. What . . . exactly?"

"Nothing, nothing." She cleared her throat and started again. "See you on set."

And with that she walked off gradually into the distance, the wind pulling at her dress and her slightly bedraggled hair. She did not even run to dissuade the rain.

Nigel roughly elbowed Stan, twice. "So . . . things are really over between you two, huh?"

Nigel had never asked him a personal question before. It was always business. Which meant the question wasn't personal. It had some business connotation, hidden in there somewhere, the words, seemingly innocent, disguising some questionable agenda. He chose to say nothing, looked straight past Nigel.

Nigel took a long look at Stan, and shifted his feet a little, looking down on the ground, as if stamping out an imaginary cigarette while an unlit one dangled, restlessly, from the edge of his bottom lip. "Listen, now is not the time to rock the boat. You need to go after her, maybe even sleep with her. Just keep her happy and onboard for a bit while I work out a few . . . things."

"Wait, what?"

"You need to go to her, maybe spend the night at her place. It's important to me that you two stay . . . *cozy*. For just the next week or so. It's important. For the good of the show."

Stan squinted intently at Nigel, as if the answer to the riddle might be written on his lying face in the kind of small print he was paying Nigel to read for him. "Why would Mary and I staying . . . *cozy* . . . be important to you?"

"Because I'm working on something. Just trust me and do what you're told."

"No. I finally just found Hope by a million-to-one chance. I'm not going to blow that now."

At the sound of hearing himself utter her name, he realized he had finally found a use for his sensory memory training, back from his acting days. He could remember, he could actually feel, the touch of Hope's fingertips, could smell the strawberry-scented shampoo she never adequately washed out of her hair, could hear the sound of her heart beating when he held her close.

"You've been spending a lot of time with that woman. What do we know about her? She could be anyone. Maybe she's just pretending to be interested in you as way to get at my money."

Stan spun on his heels. "What did you say?"

"I said, 'Maybe she's just pretending to be interested in you as a way to get at your money.' Besides, there's no way Hope would ever know."

And here Nigel stared into Stan's eyes, intently, as if trying to hypnotize him; he said with authority, "Thursdays. Thuuuuuursdaaaaays, Stan."

Stan stared at him and when no further information was forthcoming he eventually had to ask, "Thursdays?"

Nigel's hands danced maniacally as he talked, as if he were a hysterical television preacher desperately pleading with Stan to take God into his heart and send money. "Thursdays are the holy grail of television. It's feeling up the head cheerleader, it is slow dancing and grinding up against the hot girl at the prom, it is banging your friend's cougar mom. It is where everyone who is anyone wants to be. And we're close to getting the show moved there. Do you have any idea of the *money*?"

Stan noted, grimly and with no small degree of disgust, that he pronounced "money" as if he'd just had an orgasm. And perhaps he had. "If we can just get the show moved to

Thursdays . . ."

"That's great and all, but I just can't—"

"Are you a star or not? You're thinking like a person, not a like a brand. Do you want to be poor again? Do you remember what that was like? Being poor? Hungry? Having to actually work for a living? Having a supervisor? Imagine being a grown man, having someone whose job it is to supervise you, as if you might hurt yourself. And I know how you've been giving your money away—"

Stan pressed his fingertips against his forehead, hoping he could push back on the swelling pain, make it stop. "Hang on—"

"You need this to work out as much as I do. Now as your agent, publicist, confidant, notary public, friend, and owner of twenty percent of your rights and royalties, I order you to go back to her place and sleep with her—"

"But—"

"Right now!"

"This is crazy—"

Nigel poked Stan stiffly in the chest, repeatedly, as if he were hammering away, looking for a wall stud, "Stanley Ronald Pavlov, you go and fuck that nice lady right now, young man!"

\* \* \*

From the moment they arrived at Mary's apartment, after taking three quick, shallow breaths, Stan got down to business, following his instructions like the good soldier he was. If she noticed that there was an anger, a violence, a single-minded selfishness in how he took her, she had the common decency not to mention it. Neither spoke a word.

When Stan's mind couldn't help but feel a bit guilty, his body reminded him that it also felt good. And it wasn't as if he was cheating. Apart from the fact that his relationship with Hope was no more than a few weeks old, he didn't care about Mary anymore. Not now that he knew—or at least suspected—a little more about her motives. No, this was no more than a necessary work function, like having to write up meeting notes or ordering breakfast for the team when scheduling an early morning meeting or going to the company Christmas party, which was about as exciting as folding socks. No one liked doing it, no one thought of it as the watermark of their career, but it was the nuts and bolts, the bread-and-butter stuff that needed to get done so you could then concentrate on the more meaningful, more fulfilling tasks.

But this, this behavior, this feeling, Stan realized, was power. This was fame. This was why so many famous people went so far off the deep end—gambling, cheating, stealing, gorging, spending—because they could. Because they could and because it was fascinating to see how far you could take it. May the God he no longer really believed in help him, but he was starting, just a little, to enjoy himself. If only he could shake off the soft, nagging feeling of nausea and the pounding in his head, the slight blur in front of his eyes, as if he were watching it all happen on a dusty and dirty television set.

Maybe it was time to stop worrying so much. He had everything he had ever dreamed of . . . didn't he? Money, sex, fame, and something new, something he had never even dared to fantasize about before: pride.

Exhausted, he rolled off, not making eye contact with Mary, not wanting to look himself in the face, turning maddeningly away when he saw his ghostly reflection in the window. Closing his eyes tight, he focused on his breathing, as if to prove to himself he was in fact really here, concentrating on the little exploding dots that danced on the inside of his eyelids, which frantically resolved themselves into constellations, then dollar signs, before scattering away into nothing. Mary never said a word and was suffocating just a little, trying to keep her breathing as shallow and quiet as possible.

Stan heard the distinctive sound of three quick, successive rings and found himself heading toward her kitchen, without quite knowing why. He stopped when he discovered it was the sound of his cell phone ringing; the sound echoed painfully inside his head.

"Get that, will you?"

"You . . . you want me to answer your phone?"

Pulling on his bunched-up, twisted pants, Stan barked, "Yes, for Christ's sake, just stop that noise already."

"Um . . . hello?" She listened for a minute as Stan searched the room for the rest of his clothes, his glasses, his wallet. "Hey . . . Stan . . . someone named Hope is on the phone for you?"

His stomach lurched as he reached for the phone. By the time he worked up the courage to hold the phone up to his ear, all he could hear was the monotonous drone of a dial tone, sounding for all the world like the flat-lining heartbeat of a dead man.

# FOUR WEEKS LATER

# Chapter 19

Night fell like a fat nun down a rickety staircase.

It was —another—cold and lonely night. In the weeks since he had lost Hope, Stan had been fiercely saying good-bye to the man he once was. It didn't feel like his heart was breaking; his heart had gone numb. He felt nothing at all; the place where he had once believed his soul was, was now just a yawing emptiness. The sensation—the persistent, gnawing sensation—he now had was tangible. He could feel an increase in the surge of adrenaline coursing through his veins; his limbs gained a weight, there was a heightened sense of gravity every time he moved. His hair and skin felt coarser, tighter; he felt taller, like he had woken up confined in a different body and it was slightly cramped. He had grown, more out of apathy than willfully, a full beard, speckled with ornery gray. He had started using his right hand—instead of his natural left—as his dominant hand: because being right-handed had tested better with audience focus groups. But not a single tear escaped him as he lingered, curled up, night after night after night . . .

He made sure that he had a different woman, a different co-star, nearly every night: no attachments, no commitments . . . he didn't have to share his money or his time or his stage or his space with anyone. They were each, one and all, just a means to pad the time, as he numbly tore up and killed his days until it was his weekend to be with the dog again.

Stan pried open one bleary eye, tentatively, and realized he had no idea where in the name of Monty Hall he was. He must have really gotten plastered, because his mouth felt like the inside of an ashtray in a Turkish taxicab. Looking around for clues, and opening the other eye, one of the first things he noticed was the woman lying next to him.

For a sweet, brief moment he thought it was Sarah. For a much longer, painful moment, he realized he had no idea who she was. For a medium-sized moment, he realized it didn't matter.

Her apartment—assuming that was where he was—was nothing to speak of. It was an average person's home, full of paltry knickknacks to try and cover up the fact that the furniture and decorations were cheap. There were little imperfections everywhere: small scratches on the desk, tiny dings on the walls, scattered wine stains on the rug; a cleaning lady had obviously never visited. It reminded him, sickeningly, of his own apartment, way back when, before the game show gods called his name. The reminder of his past, the years wasted being ordinary and poor, made him surprisingly angry. These days, if this had been his stuff, even a small scratch on his elaborate furniture, he would have just thrown it out and bought a new one without a second's thought. He might even just buy her a new bookcase just to show off his generosity. Depended on whether she made breakfast or not.

He couldn't understand why, even in a drunken state, he would have agreed to go back to her place. He liked the idea of showing off his house, his status, his things, even to someone he had only just met, even if he wasn't particularly serious or interested in her. Like a child trying to impress their parents' visiting friends, he could imagine himself pulling out all his toys, opening all the closets and drawers, letting her admire all the stuff he and his fame had acquired.

Slowly, vaguely, elements of the evening started to resolve itself. He had been on a date . . . Stan had thought that being famous would make dating easier, but it made it even more awkward. All anyone wanted to know was what it felt like to be on television. And even though he strongly believed in honesty, even on a first date, he didn't have the heart to tell them that it was what he imagined death felt like: a numbness, a boredom, a feeling of complete emptiness where time felt like it went forward and backward at the same time, where it felt like it would never end and was already over at the same time. So instead he would say it was like having sex: thrilling, exhausting, and he felt like eating a box of frozen waffles afterward.

He tried again, rehearsed the night in his mind. He had had a date. He had had a frightening amount to drink. He had . . . he had . . . a blinding headache. Which wasn't helped when . . .

. . . she made an extraordinary amount of noise as she woke up and got undressed, removing what little bedclothes she had on. As she took off her elaborate collection of jewelry, the jangling bangles clattered on her arm. Wait a minute . . . that . . . that *noise*. That noise suddenly struck a deep and instinctive chord with Stan and he remembered: this was the woman, long before he was anybody, who had slapped his face at the bar the night that he had quit the Reflex Players Ensemble. At the time, Stan had been only mildly embarrassed by it, but with the distance of hindsight, the shame accrued interest and he was suddenly enraged.

"Well, good morning . . . Stanny Boy," she said with such innuendo that he blushed on her behalf. With just two fingers, she lightly traced two prominent veins on his forearm and his cells caught fire.

"I can't imagine how bad you feel right now," she said, without a trace of sympathy.

"I do fear my liver has handed in its resignation," he confessed. He could have her . . .

She stared at him, her lips a mere breath away from his face, daring him to make a move.

"Did we . . . I mean . . . last night . . . you and me . . . was there any . . ."

She laughed and it cut him deep. It was a laugh intended to be alluring but, like her, it was trying too hard to be something cliché and contrived.

"No . . . you were far too drunk or some of your other organs have handed in their notice as well. Shall we check?"

And with that she immediately cut to the chase with strong and unpleasantly cold hands. Stan yelped and backed away. Despite his burning interest in her, he remembered he was supposed to be offended.

"You really don't remember me, do you?"

She fell on him, like she was blacking out, her weight pressing heavily on him, pulling on his skin. "Remember you? Of course I do. You're my date every Wednesday night right here in my bedroom." And she suggestively motioned toward the television.

"But . . . you met . . . a friend of mine once. At the bar across the street from the Reflex Players Theater. Do you remember?"

"He clearly wasn't as memorable as you," she simpered as she lazily reached for and caressed his wrist.

"That's a shame. I wish you remembered him. Just a little." His puffy flesh, his bloated fat, suddenly felt cold and raw; he pulled on a taut corner of the sheet to hide himself from himself. "He was . . . someone who I admired, once. In a small way. It would be nice if I wasn't the only one who remembered him."

"You make it sound like he's dead."

"He is."

For the first time since they awoke, she stopped touching him, pulling her fingers back as if he were carved out of ice. "Oh. I'm sorry to hear that. Was he . . . a close friend?"

Stan lumbered to his cold feet, used an open palm to meagerly cover his nudity while he thought sincerely about that. "No. No, I guess he wasn't. But I felt responsible for him. And I let him down."

"Any chance I can help you forget?"

He was partially dressed, a crumple of his remaining clothes tucked under his arm. He spun to go and then suddenly, without warning, ran to her and squeezed her face with his right hand so hard that his fingernails gashed her cheeks. He kissed her hard and with contempt before spitting on the floor.

She thanked him as he bashed the door closed behind him.

# Chapter 20

Whoever said you can't go home again, didn't live where Stan lived.

It was more than a house, it was an estate, surrounded by lifeless silk landscaping, exotic-looking fake plants and shrubs that would only need simple ironing from one of his minions to look perfect, and would last forever.

The tragic joke, the cruelest irony, was that his new house—he called it a house, not a home; "home" implied a level of comfort he knew he would never feel—was spacious enough to stage a football game within but, except on the rare nights, like tonight, that he had custody of the dog, it was only, just only, him. The furniture embodied his loneliness, brought the pain to life; the empty armchair tweaked its nose at him, the lonely sofa laughed.

But tonight, he was happy; let the dog crawl, scratch, bite, whatever, on the chaise lounges, the ottomans, the armoires, anything to put the furniture to use, anything to please the dog. What did it say about Stan, he thought fleetingly, that the only living thing he might have ever loved couldn't talk back, had no ambitions, only asked for food and water, was just as obsessed with ensuring Stan's happiness as he was himself?

The dog curled up in his lap; his warmth, weight, was like a heavy, cloying blanket. They sat, in quiet, in peace; Stan couldn't bear the thought of them ever being separated again. The love in the dog's dark eyes had deepened over the years but so had the growing gray mass seeping through his fur. He tried not to notice how when he waddled now, his hind legs occasionally swerved, twitched, like the errant, rusty, back wheel of a runaway shopping cart.

Where were all his friends? What had happened to all those confidences, all the shared confessions, all the carefully laid plans, all the oaths? Eventually, they had all come to nothing. All those he had once known from elementary school, high school, college, those first early work friends, all those acting classes . . . even his family, or any one of the women he had once felt he had shared something with . . . in the end, the only one he could ever really depend on was his dog. In Stan's carefully defined hierarchy of needs, the dog's presence and love was on par with, if not greater than, any biological need; it was more vital than water, more integral than air itself, and nearly as satisfying as food. The dog was the only one who ever kept all his promises, without ever even saying them aloud.

Stan now had maids and butlers, assistants and handlers, bodyguards and chauffeurs, someone washed his laundry; an entire sub-staff was dedicated to cleaning. A barber was on-site to cut his hair at the slightest sign of shagginess. He had his own personal on-call physician. Security guards whose names he didn't even know patrolled the perimeter. The greater his entourage swelled, the lonelier he felt. When not engaged with the show or with publicity, Stan had nothing but free time, which he had no idea how to fill. The only enjoyment, the only sense of purpose left, was when he had custody of the dog.

He instructed his live-in chef to prepare marinated sirloin tips for the dog, which he was happily gobbling out of his silver monogrammed salver. There was nothing—no expense, no amount of effort—that was too good for the dog. Like Stan, the dog's happiness, his most vivid memories, the milestones with which he measured out time, revolved almost exclusively around meals.

As Stan methodically scratched his dog behind the ears, he gazed around, admired the extravagant works of art he now collected, arranged, not by period or style, but by how much they were worth: a rigid, palpable class system for his criminally expensive menagerie of paintings, sculptures, artifacts. Instead of being wasted on the general public in some clinically white museum, they were all his, trapped here, imprisoned in tiny frames, or behind the protective glass of curio cabinets, for him — only him — to appreciate. In the glass's reflection, he saw his sad, distorted image, his long face, elongated. He remembered, when he was younger, how he would study himself in the mirror, waiting impatiently for the day when he finally got taller, more handsome; that day never came.

He slumped into the bathroom, saw the more accurate reflection of himself as he prepared to get back into character; per Comb Over and Blow Dry's instructions, it was time to shave off the graying beard. Tomorrow morning, Stan would record the first episode of season two of *Animal Instinct* and he was surprised that he genuinely felt a degree of satisfaction. To celebrate, Comb Over and Blow Dry were going to take him back to the same restaurant where they had first met him. And Stan, even with his newfound fame and wealth, was not one to pass up a free meal; like a child of the Depression who later made it big, he never forgot what hunger felt like and never, ever took food for granted.

* * *

Stan, with his dog at his heels, strolled past a long waiting line, velvet ropes falling away in his wake, as he was escorted straight to his table. The same one, in fact, where he had sat way back when, many zeros on his bank account ago. As he sat down, he noticed there was a little plaque, gold-plated but tasteful, that would tell future generations: "At this very table, Stanley Ronald 'Stanny Boy' Pavlov accepted the role of host on *Animal Instinct*."

Well, that wasn't entirely true, but close enough. He couldn't begrudge this humble little restaurant for wanting to brush up against his leg, dry humping just a little bit of his fame.

"Where's Nigel?" Blow Dry asked.

Stan's bulk flopped into a chair, made the table slightly shudder. "Fuck Nigel. He can ring for his own dinner. More room for me and my dog."

Comb Over and Blow Dry held no interest for him; they were simply whiny static while he fed the dog delicacies from the table. They ranted on and on, as if he weren't even there, about points, and Q ratings, and marketability, as if he was no more than an arithmetic problem, just numbers on a spreadsheet. Their lust for money knew no bounds; he silently patted himself on the head, pleased he had done everything possible to ensure they had absolutely no access to his finances; Stan had seen enough episodes of *Behind the Music*.

Without warning, as if suddenly remembering he was there, Blow Dry turned to address him. "Stan, we didn't just want to take you out to celebrate tonight. There are a few pieces of business we would like to get out of the way."

Stan ignored them, poured the dog some more sparkling water straight from Comb Over's glass.

"We wanted to see if you had any ideas," Comb Over explained, "about what the title of your autobiography should be?"

Stan slowly drained his drink, letting the ice cubes slink down his throat and melt away before answering. "Listen, I'm sure that you think my autobiography will make us even more fucking money, and hey, I am all in favor of us making more fucking money, but you gotta understand: Stan needs to set aside some time just for Stan. Besides, barring a massive asteroid collision or you guys driving me to jump out a window, there's a lot of my story left to tell."

Blow Dry and Comb Over could hardly breathe, they laughed so hard, so long.

"Stan . . . dear . . . you didn't think we would ask *you* to write your autobiography, did you?" Comb Over gasped.

"Oh, good Lord, no," Blow Dry added. "We hired the very best in the business to ghostwrite it for you. It's already done. It will hit bookstores next month."

"Oh. Well, okay then."

"We know you couldn't possibly write it yourself. I'm not even sure you could read it by yourself."

"Ooooh. There's a thought." Comb Over jumped in. "Would you like us to hire someone to read it to you, hmmm? We could do that. Maybe just before bedtime?"

"Screw the pooch."

"Listen, we're just trying to help—"

"No, I'm saying that's what the name of my autobiography should be: *Screw the Pooch: The Story of a Man Who Brutally Murdered TV Execs.* You know, something pithy. And true."

He gave the dog another helping from the table, looked into his eyes and said quietly, so only his dog likely heard him, "Besides . . . I used to write a little . . ."

A piercing silence ensued. Stan, despite being offended, momentarily fantasized about seeing his own autobiography—with his name dancing down the spine—on a bookshelf of his library, nestled snugly between George Orwell's *1984* and Sylvia Plath's *The Bell Jar.*

By the time the waiter approached, Stan was slurring his words. Not that anyone seemed to care. Where, in the past, he would have been forcefully but politely asked to leave, now he was asked for autographs and brought free drinks.

"Mr. Pavlov, it is an honor to serve you, sir."

"Yes. Yes, of course it is."

The waiter bowed deeply, then stood at attention; Stan thought for a moment he might even salute. "What can I get for you, monsieur?"

Stan gestured to the diners at the adjacent table. "Hmmm . . . that looks good. I'll have what she's having."

The waiter clapped his hands together twice, effeminately, like a small sample-size of applause. "Ah! The Lobster Thermidor. Excellent choice, sir. I'll bring that out to you straightaway."

Stan roughly grabbed his sleeve as he tried to walk away. "No, no . . . I mean I'll have *exactly* what she's having."

"Uh . . . sorry . . . I don't understand . . ."

Stan spoke slowly, as if to a mental patient. "Pick up her plate . . . bring it over to me . . . and place it on . . . my . . . table."

"But, I . . . I can't do that . . . I'd . . ."

Stan nearly stood up, slammed his fist on the table. "Listen, punk, you sass-mouth me one more time and you'll never wait tables again in the continental United States!"

The place went deadly quiet. One or two people with no sense of occasion took the opportunity to snap a picture.

The waiter was, clearly, conflicted. He gingerly went over to the other table and quietly, as if hoping she wouldn't notice, lifted her plate limply, miserably, like a man carrying his girlfriend's purse.

The woman at the neighboring table grabbed her plate back with both hands, as if it were a family heirloom. "Hey! What the hell are you doing?"

The waiter gave her an apologetic shrug, and whispered, "I'm so sorry," as he tugged the plate away from her so hard she nearly plummeted off her chair.

Without looking at Stan, staring at the floor as if the secret to life itself was written there in bold, large print, he slipped the plate in front of Stan's grimacing face.

Stan picked up the lobster and took several loud, messy bites, broke off pieces and fed them to his dog, exaggerating his pleasure. With a full, sloppy mouth he demanded, "Take that bit off her fork, too, and bring it over."

The waiter was softly weeping now, but reluctantly did as he was told. The neighboring party was incensed, and making a lot of noise but only among themselves; no one seemed to have the courage to confront Stan.

He savored her half-chewed bite, slowly rolling it around in his mouth, "Mmmm . . . this is delicious . . . give my compliments to the chef."

"Sir, please, I must say—"

"Now!"

The waiter ran; he never returned.

Stan noticed an open-mouthed man at the adjacent table who was frozen, fork midway to his mouth, holding a perfect tableau as if he were an animatronic character at a theme park ride. He was sitting with his wife, his two kids. The epitome of the average middle-American, middle-class, middle-age man. Stan leaned toward him with a conspiratorial smile. "Go on. It's okay."

The man, finally awakened from his spell by the stench of a drunk, foul-smelling celebrity prince, blinked, swallowed and furrowed his brows. "I'm . . . I'm sorry. What?"

"Don't be coy. I know. And I know you know. So . . . go ahead."

Blow Dry put a shaky, warning hand on Stan's arm, which he simply slapped away. Stan leaned closer, menacingly. "Take. A. Picture. You're dying to. I can see it in your eyes. Having dinner across from The Stan Pavlov. Something you'll talk about and cherish for years. You lucky fuck."

The man flinched at Stan's language, like someone had dropped ice cubes down the front of his shirt. "Sorry, I don't understand . . ."

Stan, with cobra-like reflexes even he didn't know he had, snatched the man's arm and gripped tightly. He was pleased to see that the man was wincing in some degree of pain; it meant the handgrips he had been exercising with, and which now bore his name and smiling picture on the box, were working.

Stan gave a short, hard laugh. His grip tightened ever so slightly, "Listen . . . I like your style. Playing it cool. I like that. But everyone wants to take my picture. And I'm saying that it's okay, it's fine. So go ahead. I'll even give you one of my good smiles." And with absolutely no joy in his voice, he croaked, "I'm in that kind of mood."

The dog studied the exchange, arcing his head back and forth, like a spectator at a tennis match, and, like all dogs, he assumed that the two humans were having a passionate dialogue about food and how and when it was going to be served to him. Under the dog's watchful, waiting eyes, Stan got up, walked around to their table and put an arm around the wife and one of the kids. He leaned in close, stinking of a dizzying array of hard liquors, and gave his million-dollar smile. Thinking about it, he would soon have to rename that to keep up with his ever-growing bank account.

The man took his linen napkin and roughly wiped the sweat off his forehead. "Well thank you . . . uh . . . sir . . . but I don't have a camera with me. But thanks all the same."

"Well . . . your phone can take pictures?"

Comb Over looked over at the family, whom Stan still had his arms draped around, and offered a quiet, apologetic smile. He stood up and tried to gently pry Stan away. "Listen, they're thrilled enough to have met you. But let's let them go back to their meals, huh?"

Stan grabbed Comb Over by his shirt, pulled him close and then pushed him away, hard.

"No! Take my picture . . . now!"

"Now, look here, whoever you are—"

That was all Stan needed. He punched the man square in the face. Stan wasn't sure if the cracks he heard were emanating from the man's face or his own knuckles. Either way, it didn't matter, it was a satisfying sound: like the sound of applause or the imaginary *ca-ching!* of a cash register he heard in his head every time he knew he was earning another bundle of cash.

Within minutes, it was over. The man never even got a chance to throw a punch before he was hauled away by the police for disturbing a celebrity. The waitstaff quickly brought Stan and the dog another Lobster Thermidor, as his last one had gone slightly cold during the confrontation.

# Chapter 21

Outside his penthouse hotel window, the rain was angry, heavy and angry, stomping down on the glass like thousands of angry BB pellets fired from the toy gun of God. Grinding his palms in his glassy eyes, trying to stop the throbbing, Stan tried to remember what city he was in but found he had no idea. The pounding of the rain wasn't making it any easier to focus. It seemed to be raining a lot lately as if, like Stan, the sky was bitter—bitter and sad; unlike Stan, the sky wept openly, publicly, unashamed. Without getting up, or even leaning forward, he reached into the bedside nightstand and was pleased to find, right there where he had hoped they would be, his morning array of drugs. He had drugs to stop him from sneezing, drugs to smother his fears, drugs to put him to sleep, drugs to wake him up, drugs to keep him focused, drugs to make him mellow, drugs to make him more energetic, drugs to make his penis hard when he needed it, and drugs for when he didn't. Not a single bodily function or emotion was left to chance; he took them all.

As the complex array of chemicals did their jobs, Stan started to remember: he was back in New York for as brief a time as humanly possible. He wanted nothing more desperately than to be back in Los Angeles. Whatever charm he had once seen in New York had evaporated. Now that he had had a taste of other cities, of the rest of the country, he realized New York was the only place where you could do something as seemingly innocent as ordering a sandwich in a deli and have the woman behind the counter treat you as contemptuously as if you had just pistol-whipped her maternal grandmother.

Last night's flight—on one of his very own private jets, of course—had been the kind of flight where you strike a bargain with your God(s). Where prayer is not just something you recite out of habit but where it takes on true meaning. Stan had taken the Buddy Holly Special from somewhere he couldn't remember to New York City and wanted to kiss the ground when he landed. He had made a promise to himself that he would sell it at the first opportunity, that he would never board one of those little planes again. From now on, if he could reach out and touch both sides of the plane with his hands, he was out of there and whatever appearance was waiting for him could just fuck off.

He traveled so much these days it was impossible to keep track of where he was. He took great pleasure in making Nigel responsible for resetting Stan's watch every time, everywhere they landed. But very little else gave him pleasure these days.

Nigel was firmly established as his bitch now. He fetched the paper for him, woke him up in the mornings, went on walks with him when he didn't want to be alone, and stayed away when Stan did.

\* \* \*

The staff, his former fellow thespians, greeted him with deference and embarrassment. Knowing Stan was temporarily back in town, the Reflex Players Ensemble had—at long last—offered Stan a lead role. But since the success of *Animal Instinct*, he had decided to no longer consider any acting roles. If he were to appear or perform in anything, it would only be as himself. It was a thoughtless irony, that now that he could have any part in any play on any stage that he wanted, that he no longer felt the need to hide; all he wanted to be now, all he could be now, was simply himself. Instead, he asked for front-row center seats to . . . whatever it was they were currently performing. He chose to take Nigel as his plus one.

Nigel had been fidgety all night; Stan knew that meant that he had something he desperately wanted to ask. It couldn't be that he was afraid to ask Stan to do yet another public appearance or promotional tour; they both knew that in recent weeks Stan had given up all pretense of principles. He would appear pretty much anywhere at any time in anything: book signings, rodeos, mall openings, new sandwich launches, pizza parties, bar mitzvahs. You name it, Stan would hawk it. No . . . it must be something that Nigel thought he would still have some minuscule degree of principle over, something that could still offend a man who had already sold off almost everything he had. Stan was intrigued. But he was enjoying watching him squirm, so let him suffer.

Mindlessly flipping through the program, Stan recognized faces, names, and lies in the bios section; he might have once enjoyed the thrill of real acting, he might have once longed for that satisfaction of finding a real moment that brought a character to life, but he could never stand the self-obsessive quicksand that went along with being an actor: all that time and energy and effort focused on laboriously and ruthlessly spinning your own bullshit, murdering truth as if it had committed a crime against your family.

Crushing his program until it was nearly as sharp as a shiv, Nigel turned to Stan. "Listen . . . what I wanted to ask you about the other night . . . I just wanted you to know . . . I'm being given an award by the Agents Association next week."

"They have an award for agents? What is it the called, The Phonies?"

"Ha . . . that's . . . that's very funny."

Stan hoped Nigel could afford a solid dental plan on his twenty percent, because he was gritting his teeth so hard while he spoke that it looked like he was in a poorly dubbed foreign movie.

Nigel studied the remains of the crumpled corpse of the program in his hands, the ink having left black smears on each and every finger. "It's a prestigious award given for integrity and class among agents in the business."

"Really? That's kind of like being recognized as the most congenial Nazi, isn't it?"

Nigel wrung out a pitiful attempt at a good-natured laugh; it wasn't Nigel's fault, Stan thought to himself, that he didn't know how to act. Come to that, it wasn't Stan's fault that he himself didn't know how to act, either.

Suddenly, Stan turned on him. "You know, you ruined my life. Ruined. My. Life."

"Stan, listen—"

"For the first time in years, I could have been content. And you ruined it. You would have done less damage if you had simply choked the life out of me."

Nigel chomped on his fingernails, with ferocity, as if they were porterhouse steaks. "I know, Stan. I know. And I'm . . . sorry. Really. I was only suggesting what I thought was best. For you. And for the show. But my career . . . connecting people to the right role, focusing on the numbers . . . is all I have."

Nigel stared blankly again at his program, the ink and paper guts, the ads, the inserts, the leaflets, spilling over and out.

"So, about the award ceremony . . . I just thought, you know, as my second-biggest client ever, you . . . you might want to say a few words, that's all."

As the curtain rose, and the first scene unfolded, Stan let his words sink in; he leaned over and whispered, "Of course, Nigel. I'd be honored to speak at your award ceremony. It's the least you deserve."

Nigel smiled, patted Stan's shoulder. "Thanks, Stan. You're a good boy."

# Chapter 22

Last night had been yet another excruciating evening at a celebrity party, where it was nearly impossible to tell people apart since they all had the same ghastly plastic surgery look. Out of some sort of embarrassment, or perhaps as a voluntary punishment for some crime they had recently committed, they had opted to turn their faces into bland paper masks. With their eyebrows forever arched and their lips pinned back like dead, dissected frogs, their frozen expressions could only illustrate one expression: mild bewilderment—a likely expression, since, when alone, late at night, with only the comfort of their own thoughts to keep them company, they must have wondered what had made them do something so irreversible and irresponsible. What had they seen or done to make them so ashamed and afraid of looking human?

The sight of them, the thought of them, made him drink himself sick, the hangover now swilling about his head, that sour, sweaty stink that ensured that Stan couldn't concentrate on the day's recording ahead.

When he wasn't recording, Stan often found himself staring off into the distance, counting the days until his next paycheck, thinking how good it felt to see all that money suddenly appear in his bank account. His heart would race just a fraction faster, whenever he thought about all the ways he would amuse himself. It was obvious that he would never, could never, have enough now. But that wouldn't stop him from trying. He vaguely wondered, with the air of a passing daydream, if somewhere in a dilapidated attic there was a dusty portrait of him slowly getting poorer every year.

It was only during the actual recording that Stan still felt some element of regret. He still felt out of place on the set, like he didn't belong and that he was walking around in a daze. It was as if he were no longer a real person, as if he were just a disembodied ghost haunting the halls. As if to verify that he was slowly slipping away from reality, even the motion sensors in the executive bathroom no longer reacted to his movements, as if he wasn't there, as if there was no soul to register.

Dreading the moment he would have to stumble on stage, Stan suddenly smelled the familiar cheap cologne of the two-headed nemesis: Comb Over and Blow Dry. They knocked on the door, in unison, and Stan opened it just enough to let them be heard.

"Yes?"

"Stan, we'd like to have a brief word, if we may."

Before Stan could even open his mouth to answer, Blow Dry smashed his face into the small, open crack. "Now, the show is already a huge hit. So we don't want to mess with a success."

Stan shrugged. "Okay." He tried to close the door.

Comb Over stuck his foot in the doorjamb, like an old-time door-to-door vacuum cleaner salesman. "But . . . we can always make a few improvements, don't you think?"

"Well, what did you have in mind?"

"You are using a lot of colloquialisms in your opening banter."

"We'd like you to cut that out," Blow Dry said. "It limits the show's broader appeal."

Stan rested his head against the blunt edge of the door, closed his eyes, prayed his hangover would end. "But . . . that's the way I talk?"

"Yes, we know. And we'd like you to cut that out, too."

"What do you mean?"

"We'd like you to stop using your own voice."

"Not literally, of course," Blow Dry snorted.

"No, we mean stop using your editorial voice. Use the voice the writers created for you."

Stan nodded slowly, deliberately.

"Well, I have to get ready for the show now, thanks for

stopping by." And with that, Stan tried to slam the door on their faces but, once again, Comb Over wasn't so easily deterred.

"Sorry, Stan, just one more thing . . ." He'd been doing that a lot lately, like a demented Columbo. "We have a special surprise for you!" There was that oily smile again.

"What are you doing Friday night?" Blow Dry asked.

\* \* \*

Stan felt uncomfortable. This formally marked a new low, a new stage in his career. He was now among those damned tormented souls who were famous for being famous, often referred to euphemistically as a "TV personality," someone who got a lot of media coverage without actually doing anything and without having any perceptible talent whatsoever, like Ryan Seacrest or Rosie O'Donnell or George W. Bush.

So far, he had escaped public celebrity embarrassment, avoiding most of the common pitfalls of twenty-first-century fame. The only bump in the road had been a best-selling tell-all book about him written by his former dentist: *Animal Imprints: An Insider's Look at Stan Pavlov's Upper Right Molars 16-18 and 26-28 and What It Says About the Man Behind the Smile.*

But being a guest on a late-night talk show, which once had been a recurring fantasy, now seemed like a national humiliation. It was bad enough he had agreed to be a game show host—did he have to talk and answer questions about it, too? Wasn't he humiliated enough, for his sins?

"Everything okay?"

Comb Over and Blow Dry walked, unannounced, straight into his dressing room as if they owned the show, the building, him.

"What? Yeah. Yeah, everything's fine."

Blow Dry brushed imaginary fluff off his shoulder. "Have everything you need? You need a masseuse? Do you need your dressing room chair reupholstered? By the way, we made sure there weren't any green M&M's in your gift basket."

"What? Why? I like green M&M's."

"No, no, you don't."

"Um. Yeah, I do."

Comb Over held up a stern, warning finger. "No, you don't. Read your press kit."

"Wait a sec—"

Just then, the talk show's producer tried to enter his dressing room. Though, now that Stan thought about it, it was more like a royal palatial estate; sports stadiums were more cramped. After a brief negotiation over terms, Comb Over and Blow Dry slithered aside.

He tried to kiss Stan on each cheek but missed horribly. Stan thought he not only needed more practice but that it was a tad forward, considering they had just met. But the way he looked at Stan, and the way he brushed his arm as he spoke made him question whether they weren't lifelong friends—and perhaps even formerly an item? But surely he would have remembered *that* . . .

"Listen, Stanny Boy. We just want you to be comfortable and speak your mind. But don't mention politics, religion, sociology, or food. Let your guard down, but don't tell us too much about yourself. Share, but don't forget to always keep the focus on Ray. Now, Ray is going to want to say something spontaneous about three minutes and fifteen seconds into the interview. Be sure to react spontaneously and laugh at anything he says. But a genuine laugh, not a forced laugh. Play to the audience, but don't look at them. Be comfortable, but don't get too settled in. And most importantly, whatever you do, just be yourself. If you have any trouble with that, just look over at Gary and he will hold up a cue card of something that you would be likely to say. And we'll do a quick run-through just before recording so everyone knows what everyone else is doing. We don't want any surprises out there. Enjoy the show."

Gary, or at least Stan assumed he was Gary, poked his head around the corner and gave a thumbs-up, comforting Stan that everything would be all right.

"Have a good show!" And with that, the producer and Gary and his set of cue cards—which apparently knew more about Stan than he knew about himself these days—left the room.

\* \* \*

Finishing up one of his bland and interchangeable monologues, Ray was clearly pleased with himself, with the dutiful laughs and applause, apparently forgetting it had more to do with the audience obeying the laughter and applause cues than actually reacting to his material. If the jokes were so funny, why did the neon signs need to remind the audience to laugh?

"So . . . please put your hands together . . . then pull them apart and then put them together again, then pull them apart . . ."

The audience howled at this overdone routine, which Ray did every tenth show; if anyone noticed the repetition, they had the decency to not point it out.

"And join me in saying, 'Get up, come on down, and rooooooooll over!' Please welcome, Stan 'Stanny Boy' Pavlooooov!"

Stan couldn't even hear his own downtrodden subconscious over the thunderous applause. He walked calmly to the couch, concentrating on each step, believing that if he could just make it there and sit down without tripping, the evening would be a success. As Stan eased his way onto the couch, Ray gave him the obligatory Finger; Stan couldn't even fake a smile.

Stan, of course, knew exactly what Ray was going to ask; Ray knew exactly how Stan was going to respond. They had worked it all out during rehearsals. Stan was thankful that, if he just said his lines and didn't miss his cue, it would all be over in seven minutes. He was on autopilot, didn't even hear what Ray said to him, he just waited until his mouth stopped moving and then said his lines with all the conviction of a pessimistic understudy, who suddenly found himself called upon to go onstage. But then . . . suddenly . . .

"So, Stan, I understand you're quite a boring person . . . that this ordinary guy thing isn't a gimmick, that that's just who you are. Is that true? Are you really such a nobody?"

The audience laughed appreciatively and even a few jackasses gave the obligatory whoop. Anyone at home watching on a DVR, if they paused at just the right moment, might have seen a moment of panic cross Stan's face. But to the naked eye, Stan never lost a moment's composure.

He removed his glasses, with their fake lenses just for show, and massaged the divots, the little skin moats on the sides of his nose. He rubbed the lenses, took three quick, shallow breaths, and calmly put them back on, feeling far more like Clark Kent than Superman.

Stan opened his mouth to speak but Ray was on a roll. "I mean, no drug overdoses, no felonies, no speeding tickets, no affairs, not even the occasional shoplifting arrest. Just nothing. You're just . . . *nothing*. I mean, the nice-guy thing got you here, sure, and that's great, it's cute. But you're not a one-trick pony, are you?"

Again the audience cheered, hooted; a few even made noises like a dog, for some reason.

"So what . . . what do you want from me?" Stan mumbled into his chest; when he realized his clipped mike had picked it up, he repeated, loudly, "What do you want from me? Huh? You prefer your celebrities a little crazy? Is that what you want?"

Whether they cheered or not, it didn't matter. Stan made a decision. He jumped right up on the couch, bounced there, on his haunches, prancing out a demented touchdown dance. He kept it going, getting faster and faster now, and howled deep at an imaginary moon. As the audience roared their approval, Ray gave his forced, rehearsed laugh and then jumped right up on the couch with Stan, mirrored his moves.

Slightly out of breath, Ray looked straight into camera two and said, "And we'll be right back with Robert Foss from the San Diego Zoo and Samantha—"

"No!" Stan shouted, as surprised as anyone else by his reaction. He wasn't ready to give up the spotlight yet and turned his manic dance into a war cry, a rain dance, a primal, visceral statement, which he followed up by chanting, "This is my space! This is my time! This is my space! This is my time!"

The camera stayed on him for nearly a minute before cutting to commercial. When the show returned from break, the audience watching at home had missed the fact that it took five security guards to pry Stan off the couch, out of the building, and into a waiting town car in the back alley.

# Chapter 23

Stan made it a point of pride that he was never late. Being where you were supposed to be, at the appointed time, was a promise you made, a promise to be kept—even if you didn't want to be there: a third cousin's wedding, the dentist's office, inane publicity appearances, senior prom, work, proctology exams, your dad's funeral, college finals, whatever. So when Stan, dressed all in black and dragging his dog behind him, burst into his dressing room out of breath and clutching a stack of bills— with just four minutes until recording of the show started; an hour and twenty-six minutes late—he wasn't the least surprised to see the extent of unproductive pacing and smoking that was taking place on his account.

Immediately, his staff went to work, undressing him, unabashed by his patchy, pink partial nudity, then redressing him in his special brand of silk shirts, his casual suit jacket, his fake glasses, and caking his face with clumps of crumbling stage makeup to hide the lines, the creases, the newly acquired depravity.

Comb Over and Blow Dry merely stared, mouths agape, as if unsure if it was really him. Nigel's right eye twitched, winking like the iris of a thirty-five-millimeter camera; he stood up, unsuccessfully trying to hide the quaking in his knees. "And where the hell have you been? You were supposed to be here hours ago!"

Stan let himself catch his breath, sit down, peel and eat several chilled shrimp that had been specially shipped and delivered just for him, and pour the dog a bowl of sparkling water before he put his hand up, like an elementary school crossing guard, and Nigel froze. Slowly but firmly, Stan put that hand on Nigel's silk-pocket handkerchief and pushed him backward. "Firstly . . . you're in my light. Don't ever cross my light."

"But . . . you're not on—"

"I'm *always* on, Nigel. You should know that. And secondly, I was busy, okay?"

Nigel bit his knuckle until it bled. He ignored the red river that slowly plodded down his arm. "What . . . exactly . . . have you been doing?"

Stan rubbed his cheek against the dog's, leaving a wide smudge of make-up the color of a cheap, fake suntan on the dog's fur. "Well, if you must know, I robbed a bank."

"You *what*?" Nigel was literally tearing at his hair. His wispy, blond, cotton-candy fluff, disintegrating, melting away, with every pull.

"I said, 'I robbed a bank.' The dog told me to do it."

"Oh, my God, *what*?"

"I'm kidding, I'm just kidding."

Nigel gave a nervous laugh, put a calming hand on his throbbing chest. "Oh, thank God."

"It was mostly my idea. But you agreed to it right away, didn't you, boy? Didn't you? Who's my good boy . . . huh? . . . *You* are . . . yes, you are . . . yes you *are* . . ."

It was as if Stan didn't notice someone attempting to comb his hair, someone struggling to tuck in his shirt, someone desperate to smear more cover on his face to mask the deep purple crevasses under his eyes; he waltzed freely about the room, the crumbled, pale, green bills falling and flying behind him in his wake, as he encouraged the dog to feast straight from the craft services table: barbecue glazed pork ribs, caviar, foie gras, oysters on the half shell, M&M's (no green ones).

"Nigel . . . just relax. Maybe you just need to eat a little something."

"Goddamn it, Stan! Do you have any idea—"

Grabbing a slice of turkey from the catering table and dangling it above Nigel's head, just mere inches from his outraged mouth, he cooed, "Yeah, I think you're hungry. Huh?

Are ya? Are ya, boy? Come on . . . you like turkey, don't you? Huh? Who likes turkey, then?"

Nigel sneered, one side of his mouth curling up like venetian blinds when the string is tugged on. His glare was one of pure, contemptuous hatred usually reserved for extreme situations, like the hatred for a middle school gym teacher or a clumsy, farsighted dental hygienist or Rachael Ray.

Stan lightly but firmly patted Nigel's face in encouragement. "Yes, you like turkey, don't you? Of course you like the silly turkey . . ."

Stan was equal parts annoyed and impressed that Nigel was resisting—after all, the turkey did look particularly good: very moist, all white meat, crispy golden skin . . .

Comb Over slapped the turkey slice out of Stan's hand, was apoplectic: "Will you take this seriously, please!"

Blow Dry, ever the rational one, knelt softly next to Stan, as if in church, and said in an unconvincing drone, "But . . . but why? If you needed money, you could have come to one of us."

Stan laughed uncontrollably. Even the dog made a noise that, to Stan, sounded just like his own sarcastic, world-weary snigger.

"Why? Why did I do it? What are you so shocked about? Ohhhhh . . . I know . . . I get it . . . you must think I'm just a nobody. Or perhaps you think I'm boring, or that I'm just an ordinary guy. You must have me confused with someone else."

Nigel clutched his left arm, waggled his fingers like an amateur air guitarist. "Stan, at least tell us you were smart about it. No one knows about this, right? I mean, maybe you can get away with this and we'll just put this all behind us. I mean . . . you . . . you . . . you wore gloves, right? And a ski mask . . . or something? Huh?"

"A ski mask? Would you hide a handsome face like this behind a ski mask? Honestly, sometimes I think you guys don't truly appreciate me."

"Oh, my God, oh, my God, oh, my God . . . I feel . . . I feel like . . . I could . . . throw up."

And then he did. Once he had regained his composure and wiped his dirty mouth with the back of his hairy hand, Nigel whispered, "How the hell are you going to get away with this? How are you going to avoid the police?"

"I didn't."

No one made a sound. Even the dog, for just a few moments, in a dramatic pregnant pause, ceased chewing.

"What . . . what do you mean, exactly?"

Stan got down on all fours, level with the dog, and fell into his deep brown eyes. Would no one else ever understand him? Would these people never leave him alone? He answered without turning away, "I mean, I didn't avoid the police. They were on us before we even got to my car."

"Fuck my uncle with a stolen dick! Fuck, fuck, fuck!"

Stan considered signing Nigel up for a public-speaking class. Or at least getting him a decent thesaurus. His vocabulary was such utter shit.

Comb Over was calmly breathing through his clenched fist, as if it were a crinkled brown paper bag. "Stan . . . my God . . . what happened? What did they say?"

As Stan got up and stood, poised, in the doorway, he shrugged. "They said, 'Can I have your autograph, Mr. Pavlov?'"

As Stan turned to head toward set, he caught just a glimpse of Comb Over fainting face-first flat, rather effeminately, in a nearby chair. No one went over to help him.

# Chapter 24

It had taken a while but, like a brittle stick thrown to an old mangy dog, the robbery eventually came back to him. But there would be no jail time, no fines, only a small commitment to community service. Comb Over and Blow Dry and their swarm of lawyers had ensured that his sentence would have the minimal impact to the recording of the show. Their plea had been . . . had been . . . well, he had no idea, actually. He hadn't even deigned to attend the hearings; it wasn't his life to defend anymore.

Los Angeles had been good to Nigel. Instead of his skin looking a sickly white, it was now glowing a sickly orange. His new office had art deco furniture, a full staff, even chairs. It was a long way from his New York days—three stories of pretentious success, although it still had the same unmistakable and unfortunate aroma, as if Nigel had marked his territory.

Stan stared out the top-floor window; the sky was a flat, endless expanse of gray, as if the Earth were imprisoned, even suffocating, under a snug pillowcase. He had a momentary claustrophobic, paralyzing fear that maybe the sun would never be seen again.

The thought chilled him. He was distracted from this train of thought by Nigel and a flock of his helper monkeys whose names he couldn't be bothered to remember as they tried to brainstorm how he should serve his community service.

He had many strategies now to occupy his time. Today, he was calculating how many women he had slept with. Dozens of memories—of words whispered, positions, sensations, feelings, foot cramps—tumbled through his head and made him feel, by turns, giddily guilty, saddened, sickened, and delighted. In his musings, he came to a frightening calculation: he had slept with more women in the last week than in all the years before he got the *Animal Instinct* gig. That seemed mathematically improbable and he considered hiring a statistician to work it out for him. It was the curiosity that got to him. After being nearly celibate his entire adult life—or at least limited to mid-single digits, the limits of his conquests—it was that knowledge that every woman was a new and different experience, that no two were the same, that drove him nearly mad. He wondered if he would ever be satisfied until he bedded every last woman on Earth . . .

He was thinking so hard, so clearly about it, it was as if he was already there, in his stately sumptuous bed, surrounded by, engulfed by, dozens upon dozens of . . . and then that nattering fucker, Nigel, broke his concentration.

"What do you think about kids with speech impediments?"

"I think they're hilarious, why?"

The room went deadly quiet. Finally, Nigel crossed the room, in tiny, measured footsteps, put his hand on Stan's arm. "I know you're not excited about this but, considering what the consequences could have been, you got off pretty easy. So, we just need you to agree to something, put your head down, serve your time, and then hopefully think twice before trying something like that again."

Nigel knelt down by Stan's chair. For a brief moment, Stan feared he might propose; he said with intense earnestness, "But there was some good news this morning. There was another high school shooting. Several fatalities. The perfect PR opportunity. If we could get you to emcee the benefit, it might not only count as your public service but it would also really help increase our hold on the highly profitable sixteen- to twenty-four-year-old crowd."

There were mumbled murmurs of assent and excitement, everyone speaking at once, trying to be heard as the loudest, most enthusiastic, like aspiring young actors in a high school chorus. Their zeal quickly evaporated when Stan didn't react. They stopped. They sat. They waited.

Throwing his head back with a sigh, Stan tried to think of a creative swear but settled on a loud, exaggerated belch. He already worked Tuesdays to rehearse *and* Wednesdays to tape the show . . . couldn't they have figured out a plea bargain that didn't impede on his goddamn time?

One of the other dumb ass assistants spoke up before Stan could tell them all where to stick this whole meeting; it wasn't biologically possible, anyway.

"How about married moms of dyslexic toddlers?"

"Did you say *un*married moms?"

"No."

"Next."

Nigel was nearly pleading with Stan, he couldn't keep his fists from clenching. "Listen, we're all trying to help. We want to make this community service punishment as painless for you as we possibly can. But we can also take this opportunity to turn this setback to our advantage. Help ensure that you stay popular and keep the *Animal Instinct* gig for years to come. And then set you up nicely for a brand-new venue when the show finally runs its course. So once we decide on—"

"What about bowling?"

"You mean like bowling for charity or something? All the proceeds to go to—"

"No, I mean fuck it, let's go bowling. This is boring the balls off me."

"Stanny Boy . . ."

Stan's eyes dilated madly, his teeth ground. Nigel took several, shaky, shuffling steps backward across his spacious office; if he had had more grace, he might have been able to pass it off as a marginally adequate moonwalk.

"Mr. Pavlov. Sir."

"Better. Go on."

"Let's take a break from the community service brainstorm for a moment. We have a few other pieces of business to go over. We have an offer for you to do a thirty-minute infotainment."

"A commercial?"

"No, not a commercial—that would be a bit crass for someone of your stature, wouldn't it?"

Nigel laughed, snorted, looked around for some support and received none. He soldiered on, "This is an *infotainment*. It's for life insurance. You know, for pets."

"Sure, why not."

"There's also an opportunity for you—"

Stan ripped off his glasses, punched himself, lightly but repeatedly, in the eyes with his balled fists. "Yes. Just . . . yes. Just stop talking for two minutes."

"Speaking of not talking, there's one other thing we wanted to go over with you. That film script we spoke about came in. I think it's a strong vehicle for you. It's well within your range."

"Of course it's well within my range. It's a bio pic. About *me*."

"Yes, well . . . anyway, they wrote your character . . . you . . . sexy as hell. Just a few tweaks I think . . . but read it over—"

"How many pages is it?"

"Sorry?"

"How. Many. Pages?"

Nigel grabbed the script from his desk and did a quick flick through. "One hundred and nineteen."

"Tell Stevey to rip out twenty-odd pages or so and I'll do it. But I get executive producer billing, story-by credit, and weekends off. Not shooting on a fucking weekend."

"But . . ."

"I said, I'll do it." Savagely Stan spun toward one of the assistants standing behind him. "What the *fuck* are you doing?"

The assistant had foolishly dropped a pencil while taking notes, a sound absorbed by the plush carpet; no one, apparently, but Stan had even heard it.

The assistant looked around the room, from face to face, for help, found nothing but sympathetic, yet unhelpful stares. "Um . . . I was just taking notes for you . . . it just . . . it slipped. I'm . . . sorry."

Stan pounded his fist on the table, twice, like an angry, petulant Cold War Russian premier. "Don't be sorry, *think* for one fucking second! You're making noise and dropping shit while I'm trying to think and, hey, it's fucking *distracting*."

"Understood, sir. I'm very sorry."

"Do you understand my mind is not focused on my brand image if you're doing that? For fuck's sake, you're amateur."

The young man quickly put his hands to his face; if he was surprised to find that he was about to cry, he was likely the only one in the room who was.

Dusting his hands, and spreading them wide to illustrate his stance, Stan said, "Listen, you're a nice guy but you and I are done professionally."

Stan turned to Nigel and snapped his fingers; with an eerie serenity he said, "Take him out and have him killed."

Nigel placed a jittery hand on this throat, as if he were choking. "Uh . . . sorry, what?"

"Have . . . him . . . killed! When I give a goddamn command, you bitches obey me, understand?"

Nigel's knees nearly gave him away, they buckled slightly as if he considered getting down on his knees and begging. "But Stan . . . come on . . ."

"Now! Or do I have to do everything myself and take you fuckers with him?"

Stan jumped straight out of his chair, cocked this thumb back in a pathetic mime of a man holding a gun, and the entire staff jumped aside or hit the deck. Frantically, the team bustled the offender out the door, leaving Stan alone with nothing more than his satisfied sigh and a hefty sense of smugness.

# Chapter 25

Sliding his sunglasses down his long face—so he could see, it was late and dark out—Stan looked down his crooked nose at the grotesquely opulent hotel lobby while Nigel piggybacked Stan's luggage through the revolving door.

As Nigel struggled to place Stan's luggage down, handling the bags as if they were as fragile as eggshells but as heavy as anvils, Stan did a quick scan of the headlines from the newspapers that Nigel had fetched for him.

Biting his fingernails, running his fingertips across his mouth like a concert pianist, Nigel stammered, muttered breathlessly, "Anything new about your . . . about the . . . incident . . . in the headlines?"

"No, nothing . . ." Stan grunted, flipping, fighting with the newspaper, incapable of refolding a single page back to its original shape. "I think it's all blown over now. Just some shit about war or terrorism or something."

Nigel pressed his hand to his heart, as if to calm its overactive beating. "Oh, thank goodness. Bless the great Merv Griffin in the sky. Everything's fine. For now. But we're not out of the woods completely yet. Look in the entertainment section. Check the crime section, too."

"Where are we?"

"Boston. You're doing the Harvard commencement speech tomorrow. You're from here, aren't you?"

Stan's finger danced in Nigel's face, in a ridiculous parody of his own signature move, and Nigel backed away a step. "I don't know. Why don't you read my press kit and then *you* tell *me*."

"I'll . . . I'll go check you in."

Stan mindlessly flipped through the innards of the newspapers, bored with them, like he was bored with most everything. As the pages flicked by, distractedly, he caught his own name, even though it was just an island of two small words in a sea of dense print. It was still such a thrill to see his name — until he read it:

*. . . the one bright spot of this otherwise irrelevant showbiz dud is the welcome presence of co-hostess and scene-stealer Mary Schrödinger, who brings a wealth of charm and realism to this otherwise flat and clichéd pile of something grossly reminiscent of what you might carefully and unpleasantly scrape off the bottom of your shoe. The only remotely funny part of this alleged game show romp is Stan Pavlov, the host himself—who, apparently, is so inarticulate that he requires a pack of alleged "writers" to create his two minutes of pointless banter. Once this fad eventually runs its course, which is likely only a matter of weeks now, someone will happily need to put this entire herd, starting with the host himself, to sleep . . .*

Nigel came back to where Stan was sitting with a big grin on his face, like he had just done something remarkable. "All set! You're in the grand penthouse master suite! They had to kick out the honeymooning couple that were staying there, but they left the complimentary champagne and—"

Stan threw the wadded-up newspaper in his face. "Fire Mary."

"What? Are you kidding?"

"No! I'm not fucking kidding—"

Nigel raised his hands, tried to placate him. "Listen, Stanny Boy—"

"Stop calling me that!"

"All right, all right. Listen. I'm just . . . I'm getting worried . . . it's like . . . like you may come in to the studio one day and go on a rampage, killing us all, starting with me."

Stan thought about this, tilted his head slightly to the side and up, as if playing the scene out in the movie theater of his mind. "No. That's ridiculous. I'd never do that."

Nigel, as though he believed Stan was seriously contemplating it, let out the breath he was holding. "Well . . . good. That's very encouraging to hear."

"I'd be sure to kill you last, so I could make you watch."

Wrenching his sloppy tie from his neck, as if it had suddenly become a noose, he backed away. "Come on, Stan!"

"Listen. Just fucking fire her. She's a distraction."

"I know. I know she is."

"Good, then we agree."

Nigel ran a sweaty hand, hard and slow, along his crumbled, tattered suit. "Yes. We agree she's a distraction, that's why we hired her. She's hot. She *distracts*. That's what the co-hostess is supposed to do. That's what television shows do best. She's like Barbarella, drunk, on prom night. The viewers can't help but want to undress her with their eyes, imagine her doing unspeakable, depraved—"

"No, I mean she's a distraction from me."

"But the viewers love her."

Stan kicked out at an innocent table, which caused a lot less noise and a lot more pain that he had intended. "Fuck the viewers! Who cares what they think? I want her gone. Tonight."

Nigel placed a thoughtful palm on Stan's shoulder. "Listen . . . I know you two were once . . . involved . . . but let's think rationally—"

Stan openly slapped Nigel hard across his face. It made a sound like a dropped calculus book in an empty auditorium and everyone froze. Nigel stood there, red-faced, his eyes watering, which was followed by a trickle of genuine tears. Stan was surprised that he had been able to make Nigel finally feel something: humiliation. Stan could see the side of his face getting hot and inflamed and smiled as Nigel chomped on his bottom lip, as if he had a momentary child-like fear that he might suddenly wet his pants.

"Don't you dare . . . don't you dare pretend to know what I've done and who I am. I own you. You are my property." And even though the hotel lobby was so quiet everyone could still hear him, he whispered in Nigel's swelling face, "And I could buy and sell you. Now fire her."

"Yes . . . yes, sir."

Nigel held out the room key like it was the baton on the last leg of a relay race, stretching to ensure Stan didn't brush up against him as he snatched it out of his hand. Stan savagely turned on him. "You stay somewhere else. This is my hotel."

With his tail firmly planted between his legs, he slinked off and out of Stan's sight. Anyone who tried to assist Stan or offer him help or even got within his eye line, he promptly told to "fuck off" in ever-increasing volume, even if they weren't members of the hotel staff, even if they were children.

Coming off the elevator, Stan entered his room and kicked the door closed with a slam. He went into the kitchen, tore open the bottle of champagne, and drank deep. When that didn't make him feel any better, he gave the cappuccino machine an open-palmed slap—just like the one he gave that fucker Nigel—and it fell to the glistening hardwood floor, denting it. Shit, he'd have to pay for that. More of his hard-earned money just wasted. No, screw that, he'd put it in his expense report. Comb Over and Blow Dry and the rest of that faceless corporate army of the dead could jolly well pay for it.

Stan deliberately clomped around the room, knocking things over or at least making them wobble. His eye caught a splendid vase, something delicate, expensive, and worthy of respect, even in his current state of mind. He made an effort to hold it with both hands, intending to move it out of harm's way—out of his way. As he held it and felt its weight, its fragile beauty, it occurred to him: why should people be treated better than objects, than things? People were fragile, they were temporary, they were transient molecules, worth nothing. But things, at least nice things, lasted forever, deserved even greater respect, representing skill and refinement and history everlasting.

The vase meant everything to him right now; future generations should be able to enjoy its subtlety. All at once, he opened all ten fingers wide and moaned with delight as it exploded on the floor. It was his and only his to appreciate. No one else would ever have the pleasure now. The memory of it, the essence of it, would die forever with him.

Since he was already committed, he decided to give the Brazilian mahogany dresser a hard punch. It hurt his hand something awful. He hit it again. And again. With satisfaction, ignoring the burning in his knuckles and the tingle shooting up his forearm, he saw that it was splintering, buckling. Again! And again! Each punch, each shattering, splintering sound, the sound of breaking, crunching, gave him a cool, orgasmic thrill. This felt great and Keith Moon did this kind of thing all the time, didn't he, and everything turned out great for him, right? Well . . . no, actually, he was fucking dead, dead at only thirty-two, and completely penniless and alone at the end of it all. But . . . still . . . this felt great . . .

Breaking glass, the sound of breaking glass, high-pitched and trailing off slowly, still ringing in his ears ever so gently, he decided, was his favorite. After experimenting with busting holes in the plastered walls, and with tearing up all the tragic wall art— after breaking them free of their frames—he decided that, although he enjoyed that destruction, too, he would concentrate solely on glass; that would be his medium of choice. The bathroom mirror was now a jagged reflection of its former self, lines criss-crossing madly, like a relief road map of some forgotten, ancient city. The television had been particularly satisfying, initially with its sparks flying, as it was ripped from the wall, lying on its side now, staring up at the ceiling as if begging him, "No, no please!" like a minor character in a Tarantino film who had been the victim of some brutish and unjustified violence.

He had destroyed pretty much everything except the mini-bar and the snack cabinet, with its contents ten times any reasonable price and five years past its sell-by date. Frantic knocking on his locked and bolted front door was barely audible above the din he was making, but he heard it, and thought it added beautifully to the symphony of chaos he was orchestrating. The various pitches of concern, the variation, the arias of yells, shouts, commands, questions, threats created a constant backbeat to the destruction. When there was little left to break, he picked up the television set and threw it through the closed—now broken open—window, and watched it cannonball and plop gracelessly into the swimming pool below.

Standing by the broken window, gasping, lightly, for air in the breeze, he smiled. Somehow, he knew that it would always end like this, with him standing tall and high, looking down on the world beneath him, the world that was all his.

# Chapter 26

If it was warm or cold or wet or windy, Stan didn't notice. As he watched the headlights make weak little pools of light, lightly tripping off the desolate shadows, he noted how disturbing it was watching someone else drive your car, like trying to imagine someone else using your old school locker, or picturing someone else lying beside an old girlfriend or . . . or . . . watching someone else drive your car, especially when it was your pristine, custom-made Jaguar.

Stan, bedraggled, embarrassed, got in without saying a word, pressing his bulk against the driver until they slid over to the calm seclusion of the passenger seat. Before he had closed the driver's side door with an eventual slam, he was already speeding into the night.

In silence, he studied, in a dull, lulled state, the passing highway signs that hinted at other paths and adventures that might await him, if he only let himself wander. There wasn't another soul in sight.

It was the third, or maybe even the fourth, night in a row that Stan had found himself scrambling over razor-edged barbed wire, perhaps the only person in the entire state of California who was breaking in to a landfill.

"So I didn't . . . I didn't find anything—"

"Of course you didn't find anything!" Stan was surprised by the vehemence of Sarah's anger; it was especially piercing after so much quiet, stillness.

Stan hung his head and became sickeningly aware of just how bad he smelled. Spending hours at the city dump in the pale half-moon light digging through the trash, un-crumpling any scrap of paper he could find, would do that.

Sarah cupped her hands over her mouth, gagged slightly on the smell of the dump, still clinging to Stan. "What the hell did

147

you think you would find, anyway?"

Stan fiddled with visors, knobs, anything to keep busy. "There has to be . . . there just has to be . . . an idea I can build off of. So many writers in this lost town, there just has to be a good idea that someone accidently threw away."

"So you thought, *I know, I'll dig through the trash at the city dump looking for an idea*? When you offered to fly us out to LA for the long weekend, this isn't exactly what I was expecting. You smell like a skunk shat in your lap, by the way."

"Charming."

The dog barked, almost as if he were agreeing or even laughing. Stan rolled down his window, leaned out as far as he dared, fixed his gritted teeth into the biting wind, enjoying the coolness, the thrill of the air flying over and around him.

Stan closed his eyes for longer than he should have, the impression from his own headlights creating purple pixels of pain behind his lids. "I just need . . . I just need help. I've tried every creative writing exercise, every superstitious ritual. I even tried praying."

"But . . . why? Why all the sudden—"

"'Are you really such a nobody?' That's what he said. What Ray said. In front of millions. Then those bastards actually got someone else to write my autobiography. And critics are laughing at me because I need writers for a game show. And it got me thinking . . . if I could just find the start of an idea that I could sink my teeth into—"

"Yeah . . . I get it, I get it. But why the focus on being a writer all of the sudden?"

"It's not all the sudden. I . . . I used to write. When I was younger."

She neatly folded her hands in her lap, couldn't look him in the eye. "Really? You did? I had no idea. You never mentioned it before. Why did you never. . . ?"

She left the question unasked and Stan didn't bother to

answer. He had tried, as a younger man, to write. He had found that being a writer required that he have a voice; as an actor, as long as it was explicitly stated in the stage directions, he just had to do what he was told, say what someone else wanted to say. For him, the latter was far easier, kinder. He sped onward, swerved onward, as if trying to outrun his own internal, infernal demons.

"Stan . . . can you slow down a little? Maybe obey the occasional traffic law?"

"Don't you know? Don't you, of all people, know who I am?"

Stan took his hands off the wheel and looked at Sarah intently, with a glazed look in his eyes. The car lurched violently as if it were suddenly sick or drunk.

"What are you talking about?"

"I can't possibly die. Don't you know that? Don't you, of all people, understand me? I am larger than life. I am bigger than life or death or anything you can imagine. I am light itself."

"Yeah . . . to be honest, you're kind of scaring the huckleberry out of me."

"Damn it!" Stan banged his fist on the horn, it screamed in agony. "You're not listening to me! I'm telling you, I can't die. I can't *die*."

The dog was whining, begging, as if it were the only way he knew how to communicate with Stan, asking him to just stop. Sarah tried to comfort the dog as best she could with a panicked scratch. "Well, I'm pretty sure that I can, you crazy fucker, so slow down."

And with utter serenity, but rather loudly, Stan, still going far beyond any reasonable speed, closed his eyes and threw his arms straight out and bellowed, "Oooooommmmmmm!"

She tried to wrest the steering wheel away but he bit her hand, his teeth breaking skin on the fat, meaty part of her delicate palm. She let out a yelp as Stan slammed his fist, raw, three quick times, into the dashboard, until his hand looked like a half-cooked veal chop, pre-tenderized.

Sarah, bracing herself for another onslaught, tried again, placed her hands on the horn and locked her elbows, as if the alarming sound of the horn could summon help to rescue her. The horn bleated again, this time, as if it were scared, too. She cried out, "Jesus!"

Stan suddenly went limp. "Yes . . . yes, I suppose I am."

"That's not what I meant, you insane jackhole!"

He turned away, looked right at her, unaware there was even a road ahead. "You . . . don't believe, do you?"

Despite the pain pulsing inside her hand, the pain in her teeth from her clenched mouth, Sarah had to ask, "Don't believe . . . *what*, exactly?"

"Me. You don't believe in me, do you?"

Sarah, pitifully, tried to back up, scraping her feet on the floor mat. "Stan . . . please . . ."

"Tell me you believe in me!"

"Uh . . . yeah . . . sure . . . I do! Just stop the car!"

Stan punched the dashboard, elbowed his window, stomped his foot, all at the same time. "Do another take! Make it believable or I'm gonna drive us right off this bridge!"

"Stan . . . please! Think of me . . . think of the dog . . ."

"Right off the fucking bridge!"

"Stan!"

He wanted to do or say something, something meaningful, as a last possible act of existence, but he simply had nothing to say, there was no dignity of pithy last words. Instead, he simply braced himself, on purpose, and then soiled himself—not on purpose.

Sarah's fingernails gouged the leather interior, as if it would help, as if it would make any difference at all. The dog simply howled.

Stan sneaked a glimpse of the dog in the backseat, groaning into the moonroof, pleading; it made it real, scary. "Oh, God . . . oh, God . . . I never wrote the great American novel. I never went to Europe. I never paid off my student loans." He thought about this. "Well, good! *Fuck* 'em!"

Solemnly, Stan said low into the steering wheel, "And I never said, 'I love you.'"

Despite her obvious terror, Sarah sounded intrigued, "To who? To me?"

"Anyone. Doesn't matter. I should have said it. Just once. Too late now." Quietly, he repented, "Too late now."

"Stan . . . Stan . . . please . . ."

Stan jerked the wheel, hard, into the direction of the river below, which loomed large in their collective vision. Time did not slow down. Their lives did not flash before their eyes. They could not hear their heartbeats or the sound of their own breathing.

It felt like—and was—about three seconds. They did nothing, thought nothing, just went white and dumb with shock before Stan slammed on the brakes.

When her heart finally stopped pounding against her ribs, without daring to look at him, Sarah asked quietly, "What made you stop?"

"I just remembered. I have something important that I still have to do."

# Chapter 27

The night of Nigel's award ceremony had arrived. Nigel had been reminding him of it so often Stan was relieved it was finally here and nearly over with. He felt uncharacteristically nervous, just a tiny touch of stage fright. Listening to all the opening speeches, the corny jokes, the sappy tributes to those who had passed away, the has-beens reading unconvincingly off teleprompters, the mindless musical cues . . . it made him dizzy. He had a little trouble focusing his eyes, it was just a blur, a blur of noise and nonsense. Mindlessly moving into position on hearing his cue, Stan took three quick, shallow breaths and rhythmically tapped his index cards into neatness before slipping on his glasses; he couldn't see anything without his glasses anymore.

Stan coughed and began, "Ladies and gentleman . . . unaccustomed as I am to public speaking . . ."

An explosive bark of collective laughter; he knew he could have said anything, anything at all, and they still would have laughed as long as the blinking neon signs told them to.

"I was truly moved when Nigel asked me to speak at this auspicious occasion. As I'm sure you've all judiciously read in your programs, Nigel didn't always have it so easy. Looking at where he is now and the success that he's become, it's hard to believe that he started from such humble beginnings. It's hard to believe that he spent his youth not only working day and night to help feed his family but that he also spent what little spare time he had helping the even more unfortunate and disadvantaged."

Stan paused, savoring their attention, the low, warm hum of the microphone, and the contented smugness on Nigel's fat face.

"It's so hard to believe because it's not remotely true. The spoiled little cocksucker grew up with a silver spoon jammed so far down his throat he might have considered and pursued a successful career in porn if only they'd had a better health-care plan."

Pausing, awaiting a huge laugh that never came, Stan rigorously massaged the lenses of his glasses with the dangling end of his red silk tie and realigned his note cards.

"But let's look closely at Nigel's significant contributions to Western civilization, shall we? He discovered a game show host and represented a dog . . . a fucking *dog*, people. The only skill he, or indeed any of you, has is the ability to calculate in nanoseconds what twenty percent is of any given number. But you know what? I'm wrong. That's not a skill. It is a predatory instinct. A means of survival devised slowly over time to perpetuate your disgusting species."

A few people plain got up and left. A few got up but hung about in the aisle, apparently wanting to leave, but not wanting to miss what came next. And Stan, showman that he was, did not plan to disappoint them.

"Truly, Nigel is a Renaissance man of our times . . . the Francis Bacon of our generation, if you will. Now, I assume most of you are wondering whether or not Francis Bacon was the man who invented the Whopper. So let me suggest that if you ever accidentally find yourself in a library, you should look him up. That is, if you can pry your little thumbs away from your mobile devices long enough to see the world around you as your pathetic, meaningless lives pass you by."

The look, the priceless expression, on Nigel's face was reminiscent of any reasonable adult's when eating something really disgusting, like a vegetable.

"And just because I'm in the same industry as you, just because I am standing here before you this evening, I want you to know—I need you to know—I am not like you people. You think that *making friends* and *networking* are synonymous. You measure your lives in accomplishments, in arbitrary numbers, awards won, money made, places you have visited just so you can cross them off a list. What you don't get—what you'll likely never get—is that life is a series of moments, of happy memories, of laughter, noticing scenes of beauty . . . rolling around with a beloved dog. Not wasting your life giving each other metaphorical hand jobs, handing each other big lumps of metal as a reward for not doing any real work."

Here Stan had to stop and swallow hard. He felt as pale and as weak as Nigel looked, his dead, cold fish eyes staring up at Stan's, as if praying they would both just disappear.

Stan concentrated on the scribbles dancing madly outside the thin blue lines of the index card in his hand, but didn't actually see the words; for once, he had had no problem memorizing each and every one of his lines. "But I don't want you to think he is a bastard just because he would sell his own grandmother to a rampaging horde of inbred Mongols . . . because, let's face it, every single one of you here tonight not only knows you would do the same, but would compare notes on who got the highest rate. No, I want you to *know* that Nigel is a scoundrel because . . . because he made me see who and what I truly am."

Stan was surprised to find himself a little choked up, even though he knew, at times, that a dedicated performer could unexpectedly find himself empathizing closely with his role.

"Nigel Van Vliet is a bastard because he made me destroy all the false beliefs I held for myself, all my morals, my standards, my artistic integrity, my desire to be something more. I could have been happily unemployed for the rest of my life believing I really had all those things. But no . . . he handed me money, fame, success, all the things I wanted underneath and made me see who I was. I didn't like who I was . . . am. And neither should you. Fuck Nigel Van Vliet. Fuck you all."

Here he took a breath, re-tucked in his shirt, and then gripped the lectern with both shaky hands.

"And finally, I just wanted to say: Nigel, for all you've done for me, for all we've been through, after all these years . . . I sincerely hope your dick falls off while you're in somebody. You fat, smelly, pointless cunt."

And with that, Stan quietly shuffled his notes and nestled them back into the warm comfort of his inside pocket.

# Chapter 28

If they had had rotten tomatoes, they would have thrown them. Stan had committed the ultimate atrocity, violated the unwritten code of ethics among talent agents: he had told the truth.

Stan was proud of Nigel, who, just like Columbus, had apparently discovered something life changing when he least expected it: that he had a breaking point, that there were some things even he wouldn't stand for, no matter how much money was at stake. He resigned just moments after the ceremony, after everyone filed out in nearly complete silence. Nigel's resignation went something like this: "Fuck you! Fuck you! Fuck you! Fuck you! Fuck yooooooooou! And fuckin' fuck your fuckin' grandma! Yaaaargh!"

Stan almost admired him. Not for his oratory, certainly, but for the fact that he had found his line, the place where his morals outweighed his checkbook.

Stan stood at the podium long after everyone else had gone. He wanted to feel guilty about what he had done, wanted to feel like he lost an asset or even a friend, but he felt absolutely nothing at all. Maybe a small sense of self-satisfaction. Okay, maybe a tremendous sense of self-satisfaction. His speech, indeed, was the least Nigel deserved.

He was still smugly smiling about it to himself the next evening on set; it was embarrassingly rewarding to have bitten the hand that fed him. His pleasant reminiscences, his mind delving farther and farther every day into the land of daydreams, was rudely interrupted by the ghastly specters, the creeping dark shadows, of Comb Over and Blow Dry.

"Stan . . . we need to talk to you about Clara."

Stan had used his newfound and ever-increasing influence to get a month-old one-night stand—whose name, apparently, was Clara—a job as a writer on the show. Before he had read that scathing review, Stan had never really thought about the fact that game shows even had writers, but apparently they did, and apparently Stan could get whoever the fuck he wanted a job as one; it was not out of affection or kindness that he got her the job—it was simply to exercise his power.

"Listen, don't bother me before showtime. If she wants a raise, give it to her, there's plenty of money to go around. But it will come out of your salaries, not mine."

Comb Over licked his lips and tried again. "See . . . the thing is—"

Blow Dry cut him off. "Look, we know being a writer on this show isn't the most demanding of jobs, but—"

"She's just phoning it in. Literally." Comb Over said, exasperated. "She doesn't even show up anymore, she just calls into the writers' room, rattles off a few lines, and then hangs up."

Stan held his head in his hands and tried to block them out. If everyone, everything, could just stop moving, just stop making so much noise, just for a few minutes . . . a few tranquil minutes . . .

"The worst part is," Blow Dry continued, "is that she's, well . . ."

Comb Over whispered, ". . . flat-out plagiarizing. She's plagiarizing!"

Stan concentrated on his watch, and knew, no matter how long he looked at it, he wouldn't remember what time it was within seconds of looking away. "So . . . so what? So, the fuck, what?"

Blow Dry wrung his stubby hands together so tightly Stan feared they might never separate again. "Well . . . we have some degree of integrity, don't we? What do you think? Stan?"

"I think . . . I think . . ."

Stan heard the distinctive sound of three quick, successive rings—the sound of his cell phone beckoning. He checked his phone. *Oh, my God, it's Sarah. Sarah!* How many times should he let it ring before answering, "Fuck off! Not now!"

"Seriously . . . this is important—"

Stan hung up, forgot about Sarah the moment he stabbed his finger into Blow Dry's knobby collarbone. "Give her four weeks' vacation. Fully paid. Let her de-stress from the pressures of working on the high-profile, monumental, cultural phenomenon that *I've* created and I'll talk to her when she's back about professionalism and integrity."

"That's not the only thing, either . . ."

Stan snapped, leaped so swiftly at them that his clip-on mike nearly sprang loose. "Listen! Just do what I tell you, and tell her she's on paid vacation. At double her salary. Because what I say around here is law. It is fucking *law*. If I say the Earth is flat, then, hey presto, it's true."

Comb Over started to reply, but Stan put his hand roughly over his mouth, was repulsed by the scratchiness of his dry, cracked lips, which were as rough and ridged as a pair of brand-new corduroys.

"Then the Earth . . . is . . . flat. You understand me? What is the Earth, boys?"

Comb Over and Blow Dry, in unison, squeaked, "Flat."

"Fuckin' A right it is."

Stan straightened his Italian silk shirt, shot his cuffs, closed his eyes. "Hey, listen, while you're both here, there is something I need to talk to you about. I'd like to start working from home one day a week."

Comb Over and Blow Dry traded quizzical, panicked expressions.

"Uh . . . I'm not quite sure how that would work exactly . . ." Comb Over said.

"And have you even thought about my lip-sync proposal? Talking this much, bearing the brunt of carrying this show all by myself—now that Mary's gone—with all this dialogue to recite . . . it's killing my precious voice."

"Yeah, we just don't see how that's practical, you see . . ." Blow Dry said, wringing his hands, like he was trying to rub off his own fingerprints.

"Just write up an analysis of the idea and have it on my desk by tomorrow morning, okay?"

"Yes, sir."

Stan tweaked each of their noses and laughed deep. He was about to step out onstage when something he didn't even know had been bothering him came bubbling to the surface.

Rubbing his hand across his stubble-free face, Stan guiltily gawked at, spoke to, the studio floor. "Hey . . . that, uh, assistant I told you guys to have killed. Did he have a family or . . . was he just . . ."

Comb Over reached out to put a hand on Stan's shoulder, obviously thought better of it, and left his hand, hovering, delicately poised, in midair, like an absentminded conductor. "We didn't have him killed, of course. We gave him two months' pay and a good reference for another job. We knew you were just kidding, right? You . . . *were* kidding, weren't you?"

"Good . . . good . . . glad to hear that."

Stan took one threatening step toward them, growled, "But, the thing is . . . don't . . . uh . . . ever second-guess my orders again, huh? I mean, I'm glad he's okay, I guess, and it was . . . well, it was a bad day for me, but don't ever fucking cross me, you got that?"

A stagehand gently nudged Stan, letting him know recording had started.

Before he walked out onstage triumphantly, he turned around to them and barked, as if it were holy gospel, "Ever."

They had replaced the announcer several times in the last few weeks, this time with an even cheaper, less ambitious employee, but any follower of the show would be forgiven for not being able to tell the difference; like all the others, he used the same cadence, elongating his vowels: "And now, heeeeeeeeeeere's your host of

*Animal Instinct Starring Stan Pavlov* . . . Stanny Booooooooy!"

Wild applause erupted, which Stan acknowledged with a small bow and carefully blown kisses to some of the women in the front row. He had recently negotiated getting his name in the actual, official title of the show and hearing it now, it sounded *right*, it gave the show the degree of gravitas it so richly deserved.

The audience was so well trained now, all he had to do were the lackluster hand motions and they did nearly all his lines for him. He started them off: "Welcome to . . ."

*"Animal Instinct!"*

"The game show where you have to . . ."

*"Talk like an animal! Walk like an animal! Think like an animal! Drink like an animal!"*

"Sooooo . . . get up, come on down, and . . ." And here the audience roared along with him: *"Roooooooll over!"*

The theme music played on and the applause kept thumping along, the audience dancing wildly, haphazardly, as if each one was hearing a completely different song, as if all four hundred plus in the audience had absolutely no rhythm at all. It was a sea of Ellen DeGenereses out there. Stan looked out among the crowd and suddenly felt sick. They were jumping up and down like hungry seals.

He prepared to give them The Finger, choose today's three pathetic contestants, and just get this thing over with. He smoothly slipped his hand in his left-hand pocket and found his pre-show pills: a pill for anxiety, a pill for energy, and a pill for focus and deftly cupped them in his hand, plopped them in his mouth. For reassurance, he put his hand in his right-hand pocket, where he hoped to find—and did—his post-show pills: a pill for depression, a pill to put him to sleep, and a pill to maintain a four-hour erection, a regimen that allowed him to multitask his precious time, in which he could simultaneously sleep with his numerous and ravenous groupies while, actually, sleeping.

As he sighed with some degree of relief, an elderly woman in the front row caught his attention, as she was seriously in danger of hurting herself with her unfettered enthusiasm.

He cautiously approached her, refusing to come into contact with her, fearful she might disintegrate under the pressure of the slightest contact. "Hi young lady, what's your name?"

Thrilled beyond the dreams of avarice, for just a few moments, she fumbled, forgot how to speak. "It's . . . it's . . . Eleanor!"

"Hi there, Eleanor. Would you like to be on today's show?"

In response, she simply screamed and headed toward the stage, starting the arduous climb up the three hospitable stairs. Slowly.

"Come on, Eleanor, my grandmother moves faster than that. And she's dead."

The crowd was shocked into silence, as stiff and lifeless as department store mannequins, and, Stan thought angrily, they were nearly as intelligent.

"The show is only thirty minutes long, you decrepit old bat, so get a move on or just fucking die already."

The pain behind Stan's eyes made everything blurry; the audience was merely a shimmering, unreal reflection like the inverted image on a still lake. His gut rebelled, and he barely disguised a few painful retches, as his nausea escalated. A diminutive man in the front row started to come to the old woman's defense. Stan jumped off the stage to accost him. He had never walked among the audience before, he had never noticed just how much they stank of sweat and shame.

"Hey, somebody call Disneyland. I think a dwarf escaped. Which one are you, then, Dumpy?"

The audience, as one collective organism, gasped.

"So, Dumpy, what do you do for living?"

Dumbfounded, his waxen face was immobile for seconds, perhaps minutes, until he eventually re-discovered the ability to speak. "Well . . . well, I—"

"Well, that's great." Stan swiped his glasses off, clenched the bridge of his nose. "No one cares. Especially not me."

The audience started murmuring, judging.

"Oh, what? You care? Really? You don't care about anything except yourselves. Your entire lives are played out via television. Only here, could there be hundreds and hundreds of shows dedicated to nothing but making money or eating food. The only two things Americans are any good at. You people . . . you *disgust* me. You feel more affection, a greater connection, with fictional characters you've spent ninety minutes with than you do for coworkers, neighbors, and family members that you've known your whole lives. You think you're watching history and love and sadness and friendship, but it's a trick. What you are seeing are dots. Dots of dead light that lie to you."

He moved his finger frantically through the air, as if to represent each and every pixel he imagined swirling around his head. "You are all . . . we are all . . . just nothing."

The silence was absolute.

"There's nothing you won't do if someone on television tells you to do it, is there? *Is* there? All of you: jump up and down!"

They did.

"Flap your arms!"

They did.

"Lick the person standing next to you!"

They did.

"Congratulations! You've all won on today's episode of *Animal Instinct Starring Stan Pavlov* because you're all just sheep! Go *baaaaaah!*"

They did.

Several show runners, at Comb Over and Blow Dry's behest, ran out to stop the show. But Stan pushed them away and made his final announcement of the night: "And now, if you'll excuse me, while you all walk and talk like an animal, I'm going to take a piss in the aisle. Like an animal."

And he did.

# Chapter 29

Comb Over and Blow Dry, for once, were not smiling. They sat, side by side, at an enormous desk, which had nothing on it but a computer, as old, as cold, as dusty as they were. They motioned for Stan to come in without saying a word. Stan approached and chose to stand rather than sit in one of the luxurious-looking chairs, designed to lull their victims to sleep.

If he was here for his execution, let him face the music with some degree of dignity. No blindfold, no cigarette, no last-minute plea for a reprieve, just two quick ones in the back of the head. In the end, let them say of him that he faced his destiny like a man. Let the bullets fall where they may. No amount of torture would make him divulge more than his name, rank, and SAG member identification number.

When it was clear that Stan was not going to sit down, they quietly began.

"Yesterday's episode will never air," Comb Over stated with undue severity.

"We'll throw out an old repeat, and no one ever need know of this," Blow Dry added without looking directly at Stan; he peered, squinting, into the depths of his computer screen.

Comb Over apprehensively brushed aside one stray hair, meticulously placing it back among its two reliable brethren. "Hopefully, we can pay off the people in the audience today to just keep quiet."

And here, as if on cue, they both looked directly at Stan, unblinking, unfaltering, as they prepared to pass sentence. Suddenly, it felt as if the floor fell out from beneath him; it had all become terribly real.

He would repent. He would make a public apology, circulated to every major media outlet. He would declare that it was all taken out of context. That it was just a joke. A pun. He would try and draw sympathy from the public by pointing out how the crew had betrayed his trust if the footage of his blow-up ever leaked . . .

"As of Monday, based on yesterday's performance, *Animal Instinct Starring Stan Pavlov* will be canceled. You will receive a check at the end of the week, a fifty-percent buyout of your contract through the rest of the season."

Stan very slowly eased himself into the chair (*hey, this is pretty damn comfy*). What had he done? What the *hell* had he done? He had money, fame, adoration, women, power, everything he had ever wanted and he threw it all away . . . and for what? Principles? What the hell were they worth? Who in the vast and complex recorded history of mankind was ever remembered for their principles? If only he could go back, do just one more take . . .

"Starting next month, you'll start recording your own hour-long, late-night cable talk show." And at that, Comb Over finally smiled. "Vicious and painful pranks, crass nudity, taunting young women with no self-esteem, insulting the studio audience, hanging up on viewers who call in, celebrity gossip, interviewing reality show train wrecks, you know the kinda thing."

"Five nights a week," Blow Dry added. "Broadcast live. In over a dozen countries. Congratulations."

Blow Dry held out a limp, pink palm but Stan merely stared. He realized he hadn't taken a breath for well over a minute and suddenly let out a somewhat panicked gasp.

Unembarrassed, Blow Dry put his hand down and lightly patted the table. "Let's just hope no one from the audience gives the game away."

"Would be a shame," Comb Over wheezed. "If we can just keep the transformation of America's most mundane game show host into television's filthiest, darkest, meanest TV personality a secret until the pilot airs, ratings will hit the roof."

"We will kill during sweeps." And Blow Dry licked his lips.

"Now, you'll be making about ten times more money," Comb Over said.

"But," Blow Dry jumped in apologetically, "there will be bonus incentives based on ratings points so, you know, that number could jump up significantly."

Stan was in a daze. If he had sold his soul to the devil, he had forgotten all about it. He just hoped, when his fateful day finally came, there was a workable loophole. Either way, he was going to enjoy it as long as it lasted. He'd take up illicit drug use; it seemed to always get a bad rap, but how could so many celebrities be wrong? He would buy far more cars than he needed. He would build an addition on his house just for drinking—a whole wing stacked with booze and rubber-rimmed furniture so he couldn't hurt himself. And he would definitely—definitely!—get himself a gaggle of loose women to just hang around the house, waiting, available at his beck and call . . .

He would get plastic surgery. He would remake his face into a clean and empty slate. No more lines, no marking of time, no trace of ethnicity, no sense of humanity. His face would be a timeless, frozen monument to success; he owed it to his public to stay the same beloved statuesque figure forever and forever.

He would maybe even do something, to give a little back to the world that had been so good to him, like adopt a sick kid from some horrible country God had clearly forgotten about. He would give him some wonderfully pretentious name, something that would maybe be even more embarrassing than the plight that Stan's generosity had saved him from, but he would grow into it, learn to appreciate it. He could picture him now, with a belly swollen round and warm like a little sun, with a dozen flies like satellites, like moons, orbiting around him as if by some uncontrollable force. Stan would never touch or talk to it, of course, but it would be ever so grateful . . . and he would be one step closer to securing his sainthood . . .

He might even allow himself to be nominated for president.

He would have less influence than he had as a game show host, but just think of the audience, the exposure. Maybe he would put his image on a commemorative stamp. Or, he had always thought, he had a regal profile ideal for coinage. Hell, he was president, he could do both.

Stan stood up, feeling his way along the wall, floated toward the door. If this was indeed all real, then he had work to do.

"So, uh, we'll just work out the details with Nigel?" Blow Dry called out to him.

"Yeah, yeah, whatever, that's fine," Stan mumbled before he realized what he just said. He turned around and gave them both the first genuine smile he had ever graced them with. "No, actually, not through Nigel, no. Just make the checks out to me. All for me."

And then, more for himself than for those two douceberries, just because he really liked the way it sounded, he softly repeated, "All for me."

# Chapter 30

For the first time in a long time, Stan felt good. Really good. Recently, he had shunned public places, tired of the stares, the gasps, the smells of the common man; he spent so much of his time locked inside these days that the blistering light of the pale, yellow sun itched and prickled his skin. He had preferred to be alone, safe, secured and isolated, bound in a nutshell—the confines of his princely, guarded mansion—and count himself a king of infinite space. But now, the world was officially his kingdom and today he decided he would take a long, slow walk in the park. He wanted to walk among his adoring public one last time before his new persona took flight. Who knows, they would probably love and worship him even more now. After all, who in twenty-first-century America didn't worship a man who publicly insulted and humiliated them?

He was going to become a *God*. And not a wishy-washy, metaphysical, *invisible man in the sky, gee, I hope you're really there* God; he was going to be a powerful, all-knowing, vengeful, influential God, altering people's very thoughts and ideas and behaviors, people would emulate his every nuance, repeat his catchphrases like a solemn call-and-response prayer, he would magically appear in millions of homes simultaneously. *That* was what it meant to be a God, motherfucker!

On some far-flung day that awaited him in the distant future—when he was ready to retire and while away his twilight years with celebrity game show cameos, fan convention appearances, and product endorsements—he imagined that the general public would erect a timeless statue to honor him, twenty, maybe thirty feet high, trying to replicate the sheer presence his persona radiated. There might be a long line of younger, hungrier leading men that wound around an imaginary and metaphorical block, ready to push him aside and step straight into his still warm shoes, but no amount of youthful good looks could or would ever really replace what he had. He had poise. He had grace. Even in some sci-fi future generation, when robotics made every other human skill and effort deathly obsolete, he knew what he possessed and contributed to recorded antiquity was unique, inimitable human genius that would be celebrated forever. And maybe, someday, he might even die, but his fans had nothing to fear; he would be VIPed right past the velvet ropes and be given a special throne in heaven from which to entertain as well as pass judgment, in his infinite wisdom and showmanship.

The park was the great equalizer. He hummed happily as he watched the hordes of homeless shiver and burrow for scraps; the public park was just as much theirs as it was his. In his own small way, he envied those smelly, dirty little crumples of filth: they had no demands, no expectations, no pressures. They could do anything they wanted, any time they wanted. Sadly, no such salvation awaited Stan; such was the price of stardom.

It didn't take long for him to be spotted and soon he was lounging casually on a park bench signing autographs for a line that stretched past the conservatory, the botanical garden, the lake, and all the way down to the children's zoo.

A beautiful little boy, with big, dumb cow eyes and a toothless smile straight out of central casting, and dragging behind him a small puppy with soft, beautiful fur the color of melted chocolate, approached Stan with his battered school notebook and a well-chewed magic marker. The boy looked remarkably, frighteningly, similar to how Stan had looked at that age—slightly wavy blond hair, chubby cheeks, bright eyes. His mother stood proudly beside him, and just . . . just because . . . he gave her a solid *attagirl* slap on her Sunday-morning-yoga-firm ass. It still astonished him that a total stranger—if he were on TV—could get away with something like that. Not only wasn't she calling the police and swatting him with her handbag, but she was quietly giggling, blushing, probably thinking how she would tell all her friends that Stan Pavlov—*the* Stan Pavlov!—had actually touched her.

*But wait, maybe that's it,* Stan thought. *She doesn't think of me as a total stranger.* Once a week, there he appeared, thirty-six inches high, right in her living room, dancing around inside that magic little box, like clockwork, perhaps one of the only dependable things she had in her life.

As he scribbled his name in the kid's notebook—an illegible doodle that said simply, "Stanny Boy"—he was struck again by what a strikingly innocent and moving face the boy had. It was a shame there were so many damn child labor laws and regulations, he thought regretfully. He could make an obscene fortune representing this kid. He conjured up vision after vision: cigarette ads with the boy holding a long menthol in one hand and a crayon in the other. Whiskey would fly off the shelf with this kid's little red face on the bottle. Pooper-scooper refill bags, pesticides, roach motels, deodorant, colored toothpicks, throat lozenges, fake plastic dog poo, urinal cakes, travel-size cotton squabs, breath mints for pets, spray cheese in a can, all the glorious wonders of modern civilization . . . he could build up a marketing empire by exploiting the shit out of this kid. Think of all that money rolling in . . . the money . . . green and crinkly with that enticingly delicious aroma, smelling faintly of mold and mildew, that intoxicating smell . . .

It was impossible to believe, to even remember, that there had ever been a time when everything didn't fall his way: when he couldn't land an acting job, when a woman could ever break his heart, when he could have ever contemplated ending it all by driving off the end of a bridge.

Life, at long last, was perfect.

Stan heard the distinctive sound of three quick, successive rings—the sound of his cell phone beckoning; *goddamn it . . . Sarah . . . again . . .*

Primarily to entertain and enjoy himself, he made a point of doing a big, hammy eye roll, which was followed by an exaggerated, exacerbated sigh. "What, Sarah? What the hell do you want? You have to stop calling me."

"I just flew in, just landed in LA. I need to talk to you . . . in person . . ."

Stan unrolled himself, lazily, on the bench, stretching out, unfolding his legs, claiming the territory as his own. "Listen, I'm sorry, it's too late to try and get back together. You had more than enough chances. I know I told you that I'd take you back, but things have changed . . . *I've* changed and you need to know—"

"Stan . . . please. Just listen. It's your dog . . . "

"I know, I know . . . I missed the last few visits, but just tell him—"

"He . . . he *died*, Stan. Your dog . . . I'm sorry . . . I really am sorry, but . . . he's dead. If it helps at all, it was quick. He didn't suffer. I was with him. I held him. He . . . he almost, nearly, smiled. I tried to tell you the other day when I called but . . ."

Maybe Stan noted a change in her voice, in her pitch, the agonizing labor of holding back tears, strangling sobs. "I knew you would want to be with him, so . . . but—"

If Sarah had anything else to add, Stan didn't hear it. His phone shattered as he dropped it on the heartless pavement.

# Chapter 31

From eight stories up, even Los Angeles seemed like a small, quiet town as Stan looked down through the brownish, bluish, yellowish smoggy sludge that passed for air out here. How was it allowed to get like this? Stan knew he had truly wasted his life, that his time would have been better spent trying to save the planet, trying to leave the world just a little better than he had found it. Fighting to make the air cleaner. Fighting to wipe billboards from the face of the Earth. Fighting for an end to violence. Maybe next time around he would make more of himself. Assuming there was a next time around. Oddly, this was not the most pressing matter on his mind, though, as his size-nine wingtips hung over the outside ledge of his master bedroom window.

This was not how he had pictured it all ending. He had always imagined he would live well into his nineties and then be smothered to death beneath several dozen busty ladies of various ethnicities and backgrounds. A tad unrealistic, perhaps, but it was a premonition that ensured he never feared his own death.

Which left him completely unprepared for this moment. It had been such a fast turnaround, from nothing to fame and then . . . emptiness. At a moment like this, some degree of belief would have nice. A belief that someone, or some power, would save him. That he would be told what to do. That everything would maybe turn out all right. He shut his eyes tight and threw out his arms, listened hard. He waited for a sign, listened for his cue. But, no . . . nothing. Nothing came.

The reality of the situation suddenly hit him, physically. Like most East Coasters who relocate to Los Angeles, Stan was surprised how cold it could get; he was shivering on the window ledge, a chill breeze blowing. Stan remembered it was already the start of winter: December 27. Seemed like as good a day as any to die on. He pictured how December 27 would look on his headstone and then it occurred to him—with no close family, no girlfriend, no friends, not even an agent—who would get that headstone made? No one. No one would . . .

This was a moment he wanted to experience privately, quietly, but there was already a media circus spinning below him; it was too much commotion for a nobody suicide attempt, someone must have recognized who he was. But how the hell had someone recognized him from eight stories below? There was truly no hope of escape from his public anymore.

And, of course, the usual supporting cast had all been tipped off somehow and were standing by his bedroom window shouting various clichés of support: Sarah, Mary, Hope, Comb Over, Blow Dry, even a silver-haired priest. Not Nigel, though. Must still be mad. Good for him. Seriously. Stan admired people who could still commit these days.

Sarah had the first line in this scene as she muscled her miniscule way to the front. "Stan! If you won't think of me, or think of yourself, think of your poor little dog . . . do you think he'd want this?"

The dog. The mere mention of him made Stan ache for the old days, for the person he once was. But the man who was capable of loving that dog was already long since dead. And this new person, merely capable of grieving for that dog, was not far behind.

Sensing his moment, the priest positioned his face through the small window opening. "Stan, please listen to me! Please try to understand. Life is the most precious thing there is. When you're alive, when your eyes are truly open, only then can you see the unerring beauty of life. Even when suffering, to know that there's so much wonder still to discover. To be able to look up and study the infinity of the stars or to see the improbable perfection of God in the petal of a wildflower . . . well, when you're living life on that level, you'd gladly suffer sometimes to greedily take every second God gives you."

For the first time, Stan craned his cramped neck toward the window, caught just a glimpse of the ensemble behind the curtain. "Wow, Father . . . that was . . . beautiful. I've never seen the world in that light before. Just one thing confuses me, though . . . I'm Jewish, so . . ."

Stomping off in anger, the priest shouted over his departing shoulder, "Oh, fucking hell! God*damn* it . . . waste my goddamn time . . ."

"I'm . . . I'm sorry, but . . ."

After the priest's slamming of the door, there were a few protracted moments of utter and profound silence. In the hushed awe of the disheartening quiet, Stan suspected he vaguely heard Comb Over and Blow Dry frantically on the phone, tying off loopholes in his contracts.

Blow Dry gave Sarah a gentle nudge. "Go on. Say something. He needs you right now."

She exhaled, tugged on the frayed edges of her hair, tried again. "Stan! Don't do it! Please don't jump! I'm . . . I'm pregnant!"

Nearly slipping, grasping for the crumbling brick with the edges of his fingernails, Stan said, "What? Really? Wait . . . wait a minute, that doesn't make any sense . . . we haven't been together for years."

"Well, no . . . it's not *yours*, but I just thought you should know."

"Now? You thought I should know *now*?"

"Give me a break . . . I haven't had to talk someone off a ledge before!"

"Yeah, well, don't quit your day job—whatever that is—I don't really think you're cut out for it, do you?"

As often happens during the first off-book run-through, cues were sloppy, hanging on the air. With everyone waiting on what Stan would do next, he finally had what his parents always wanted from him: silence.

The air was feeling thin in his lungs. "I'm . . . I'm scared. I'm really scared. Someone . . . take my hand . . . please."

Someone did. He didn't know who did and it didn't matter. Stan just needed one last moment of human connection.

Mary picked up her cue and went next. "We never did get to watch the sunrise, did we?"

"No. No, I guess we didn't. Yet another promise I didn't keep."

"There's still time, you know . . ."

Stan slowly shook his head. At that, Hope seemed to sense, in a way the others hadn't yet, how real this was. "Do you have any . . . is there anything . . . I mean, would you prefer . . ."

He knew what she was asking. "Cremated. Please have me cremated. And scattered. Anywhere, it doesn't matter where. I was never here. Let's all just pretend I was never here."

Then, everything went silent for a moment. The silence where you can hear the wind in your ears, the sound of your lungs expanding and contracting. It must have been a sensation they all experienced at once, because suddenly he saw everyone go white. Hope leaned out farther than she should have dared and asked, as if sensing there might be no going back, "Stan? Do you have any regrets?"

It was as if the question knocked the wind out of him. "Yeah. Yeah, I do . . ."

Hope leaned out just a bit farther, afraid he had spoken so softly she had missed what he said. Just at that moment, a flock of birds flew past, making such a startling noise, it sounded as if they were laughing at him, as if they knew what he was going to say.

"Everything. I regret . . . everything."

No last words came to him. As if his life could be summed up in a single, pithy phrase anyway. He shuffled three millimeters closer to the edge; on a window ledge, that is a pretty serious step. His entourage gasped, knowing it was time to pull out all the stops.

Sarah stood on tiptoe, leaned out farther, the cold, careless wind brutally blasting the hair from her forehead; her pale face looked like she might be sick. "Stan . . . just . . . don't. Just don't . . ."

But Sarah's sentence remained unsaid; Stan jumped.

# Chapter 32

As Stan fell, the Earth below rising to meet him as if to give him a warm embrace, his life flashed before his eyes. It consisted mostly of waiting: waiting to go to school, waiting to move out of his parents' house, waiting to pay off his mortgage, waiting to get his big break, waiting to make it big, waiting to retire, waiting to find true love.

But whatever it was he had been really waiting for, now would never arrive.

It was only an eight-story fall and sometimes, miraculously, people survive stuff like that. But no, in this case, Stan was just dead. His last word, his dying word, had simply been the dog's name, whispered quietly and carried away on the wind.

I would like to sincerely thank Gotham Writers Workshop NYC, and, in particular, Lev Rosen: outstanding author, mentor, *mensch*. It is certainly no hyperbole to say that this book would not exist without his encouragement, enthusiasm, and constructive criticism.

# Roundfire

# FICTION

Put simply, we publish great stories. Whether it's literary or popular, a gentle tale or a pulsating thriller, the connecting theme in all Roundfire fiction titles is that once you pick them up you won't want to put them down.
If you have enjoyed this book, why not tell other readers by posting a review on your preferred book site. Recent bestsellers from Roundfire are:

### The Bookseller's Sonnets
Andi Rosenthal

*The Bookseller's Sonnets* intertwines three love stories with a tale of religious identity and mystery spanning five hundred years and three countries.
Paperback: 978-1-84694-342-3 ebook: 978-184694-626-4

### Birds of the Nile
An Egyptian Adventure
N.E. David

Ex-diplomat Michael Blake wanted a quiet birding trip up the Nile – he wasn't expecting a revolution.
Paperback: 978-1-78279-158-4 ebook: 978-1-78279-157-7

**Blood Profit$**
The Lithium Conspiracy
J. Victor Tomaszek, James N. Patrick, Sr.

The blood of the many for the profits of the few… *Blood Profit$*
will take you into the cigar-smoke-filled room where American
policy and laws are really made.
Paperback: 978-1-78279-483-7 ebook: 978-1-78279-277-2

**The Burden**
A Family Saga
N.E. David

Frank will do anything to keep his mother and father apart. But
he's carrying baggage – and it might just weigh him down …
Paperback: 978-1-78279-936-8 ebook: 978-1-78279-937-5

**The Cause**
Roderick Vincent

The second American Revolution will be a fire lit from an
internal spark.
Paperback: 978-1-78279-763-0 ebook: 978-1-78279-762-3

**Don't Drink and Fly**
The Story of Bernice O'Hanlon: Part One
Cathie Devitt

Bernice is a witch living in Glasgow. She loses her way in her
life and wanders off the beaten track looking for the garden of
enlightenment.
Paperback: 978-1-78279-016-7 ebook: 978-1-78279-015-0

## Gag
Melissa Unger

One rainy afternoon in a Brooklyn diner, Peter Howland
punctures an egg with his fork. Repulsed, Peter pushes the plate
away and never eats again.
Paperback: 978-1-78279-564-3 ebook: 978-1-78279-563-6

## The Master Yeshua
The Undiscovered Gospel of Joseph
Joyce Luck

Jesus is not who you think he is. The year is 75 CE. Joseph ben
Jude is frail and ailing, but he has a prophecy to fulfil ...
Paperback: 978-1-78279-974-0 ebook: 978-1-78279-975-7

## On the Far Side, There's a Boy
Paula Coston

Martine Haslett, a thirty-something 1980s woman, plays hard on
the fringes of the London drag club scene until one night which
prompts her to sign up to a charity. She writes to a young Sri
Lankan boy, with consequences far and long.
Paperback: 978-1-78279-574-2 ebook: 978-1-78279-573-5

## Tuareg
Alberto Vazquez-Figueroa

With over 5 million copies sold worldwide, *Tuareg* is a
classic adventure story from best-selling author
Alberto Vazquez-Figueroa, about honour, revenge and a
clash of cultures.
Paperback: 978-1-84694-192-4

Readers of ebooks can buy or view any of these bestsellers by clicking on the live link in the title. Most titles are published in paperback and as an ebook. Paperbacks are available in traditional bookshops. Both print and ebook formats are available online.

Find more titles and sign up to our readers' newsletter at
http://www.johnhuntpublishing.com/fiction

Follow us on Facebook at
https://www.facebook.com/JHPfiction
and Twitter at https://twitter.com/JHPFiction